Maybe it was the sight of Mitch with his tie tugged off and the first few buttons of his white shirt opened.

Maybe it was her reaction to the black chest hair peeking out. Maybe she thought about all he'd done for her.

Maybe, for just a short time, she gave in to the thought that she might *need* a protector. She only knew thoughts weren't running through her brain as fast as heat was flashing through her body.

Lily wasn't thinking at all when she leaned forward.

Rather, she was feeling and wishing and hoping and remembering what it had felt like to be held in a man's arms.

Dear Reader,

Veterans are close to my heart. My father-in-law served in World War II. My dad was a soldier then, too. These men were honorable, brave and quiet about what they'd experienced.

My hero, Mitch Cortega, an Iraq War veteran, has scars that are deeper than the physical. Only opening his heart to my heroine, Lily Wescott, can begin the real healing process. A widow from the Afghanistan War, Lily wants to stand on her own with her newborn twins. Yet she needs Mitch's inherent strength. Together Lily and Mitch realize that love truly can conquer all.

I hope you become as deeply involved in this romance as I did writing it. I hope you are uplifted by the power of love.

All my best,

Karen Rose Smith

TWINS UNDER HIS TREE

KAREN ROSE SMITH

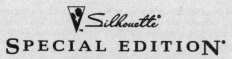

SPECIAL EDITION

Published by Silhouette Books

America's Publisher of Contemporary Romance

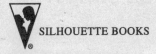

SILHOUETTE BOOKS

ISBN-13: 978-0-373-65569-4

Recycling programs
for this product may
not exist in your area.

TWINS UNDER HIS TREE

Printed in U.S.A.

Books by Karen Rose Smith

KAREN ROSE SMITH

Award-winning and bestselling author Karen Rose Smith has seen more than seventy novels published since 1992. She grew up in Pennsylvania's Susquehanna Valley and still lives a stone's throw away with her husband—who was her college sweetheart—and their two cats. She especially enjoys researching and visiting the West and Southwest where her latest series of books is set. Readers can receive updates on Karen's releases and write to her through her website at www.karenrosesmith.com or at P.O. Box 1545, Hanover, PA 17331. Readers can also visit her fan page on Facebook.

To my father-in-law, Edgar S. Smith, who served in
World War II in Patton's army. We miss you.

For all servicemen who strive to keep us safe.

Thanks to Captain Jay Ostrich,
Pennsylvania National Guard,
who so readily and patiently answered my questions.
I couldn't have developed my hero's character
so deeply without his input.

Chapter One

Late February

Dr. Lily Wescott stood at the podium, peering through the spotlight into the sea of faces in the hotel ballroom. Many grinned and waved as she prepared to accept the Medical Professional Woman of the Year Award.

She brushed tears away, stunned and totally overwhelmed. These days, she blamed the rise and fall of her emotions on her pregnancy, though memories of the husband she'd lost in Afghanistan were never far from her heart.

Suddenly an odd sensation gripped her back and a cramp rippled through her stomach. As best she could, she fought to keep her shoulders back and a smile on her face. She couldn't go into labor now! She was only at thirty-three weeks.

But she was an ob/gyn—and she knew all too well that her twins would come when *they* were ready. Lily could only hope for the best....

"Thank you," she said into the microphone. "I never imagined I'd win this award." She'd really expected one of her friends at the table to win. After all, they were all baby experts at the Family Tree Health Center in Lubbock, Texas. She went on, "At the Family Tree Fertility Center, we strive to help women who—"

A second cramp squeezed Lily's side and she caught the wooden podium for support. Out of the corner of her eye, she saw her friend and colleague, Dr. Mitch Catega, jump to his feet, concern on his face. He rushed to the stage and up the steps.

As she managed to suck in a gulp of air, hot liquid washed down her leg. *Oh, God—I am in labor!*

She was *not* going to panic. She was *not* going to crumple to the floor. She was *not* going to be embarrassed.

At her side now, Mitch's arm curled around her waist...his injured arm. *The one he never let anyone see,* she thought, needing something other than the pain to concentrate on. His arm was always covered, tonight by a well-cut black tuxedo that made his shoulders seem even broader than usual. She'd noticed that tonight... and it wasn't the first time...

"Can you walk?" he asked, his breath warm at her ear.

A murmur swept through the audience.

She turned, the side of her cheek brushing his chin. "I'm not sure."

Mitch's angular jaw tightened, his almost-black gaze held hers with...something she couldn't define. But then it was replaced by the empathy and compassion she'd felt from him many times before. "The twins are our main priority. Hold on to me if you can't stand on your own."

She really thought she could. The cramp faded away. If it weren't for the wetness between her legs, she could deny what was happening.

With Mitch's arm still around her, she took a couple of steps. Maybe she could even give the rest of her acceptance speech—

The lance of pain that pierced her back stole her breath and weakened her knees. She exhaled, "Mitch…"

And he was there…lifting her into his arms…carrying her down the dais steps.

"I'm driving her to the hospital myself," Mitch said, as Lily's friends and colleagues rushed toward him. "It will be quicker than waiting for an ambulance."

"And more economical," Lily realized aloud, trying to think practically. But that was difficult with Mitch's cologne reminding her of the last time he'd held her so close on the day she'd discovered she was having twins. His grip felt safe now as it had then…as if no harm could come to her while she was in his arms.

She must be delusional.

"I'll ride with you," Jared Madison offered as he jogged alongside Mitch and pushed open the ballroom door. "I'll be handy if the twins won't wait, since Lily's doctor is at a conference."

Jared had his own obstetrical practice at Family Tree but took turns covering with the doctors in *her* practice. Lily knew and liked Jared and felt comfortable with him. Still, she murmured, "They'd darn well better wait. It's too early. They'll be too small!" Her last words almost caught in her throat and her bravado deflated.

In the middle of the hotel lobby, Mitch stopped. Looking her directly in the eye, he said, "If you panic, Lily, you won't help the babies. Take calming breaths. You can do this."

Her heart felt lighter, as if Mitch was really part of this pregnancy, too. Not just because her husband had asked him to watch over her but because he *cared*. "If I'd taken the childbirth classes this month instead of next—" She'd been putting them off, maybe trying to deny the inevitable—that yet again, her life would be altered in an earth-shattering way.

"The twins would still come early," he reminded her. "They apparently want to meet their mom *now*."

Yes, they did. And she wanted to meet *them*. She couldn't wait to hold them and tell them how much she loved them. How much their daddy would have loved them…

Mitch's expression was gentle, as if he could read her thoughts, but his gaze didn't waver. His arms were so strong. For a moment, she felt a little trill of excitement in her chest. But that was because of the babies—wasn't it?

"Let's go," she whispered, shaken by the emotions she didn't understand.

Mitch paced the maternity floor waiting room and stopped when he saw Lily's friends watching him peculiarly. He didn't like the worried expressions on their faces. Raina, Gina and Tessa were all baby experts. Along with them, he knew premature babies often had problems—thirty-three weeks was iffy.

Trying to loosen up the tight feeling in his shoulder, arm and hand—injuries that reminded him all too often of his service in Iraq—Mitch flexed them, then sank down on one of the vinyl chairs.

Moving forward on the sofa, Tessa said gently, "It really hasn't been that long."

What was worrying Mitch was that they hadn't heard anything in the hour they'd been here. Closing his eyes, he remembered the day Lily had learned she was having twins. It had been the week before Thanksgiving. One of the techs in the office had performed the ultrasound. Mitch had just finished discussing fertility procedure options with a couple. As his clients had headed for the reception area, he'd noticed Lily exit the exam room, her complexion almost sheet-white, her blue eyes very bright.

"The ultrasound go okay?" he'd asked.

"Oh, Mitch, I'm having *twins!*"

He hadn't been able to tell if she was totally elated or totally terrified.

Clasping her hand, he'd pulled her into the office he'd just vacated. "What's going through your head?"

She'd stood at the chair in front of his desk, holding on to it for support. "The obvious. I'll be a single mom. My friends all say they'll help, but these babies will be *my* responsibility."

"Twins will always have each other," he pointed out. "They won't grow up lonely. They'll be able to play together." He hoped Lily could see the upside of this monumental news. "Girls or boys?"

"They're girls."

"Our techs are pretty good at distinguishing the difference."

Lily had actually blushed a little. Until he'd met her, he didn't think women blushed anymore. But she was blonde with fair skin and all of her emotions seemed to show in her complexion. Major ones had played over her face over the past few months—grief, fear, determination and the sheer loss of her husband.

"Troy would be so proud," she'd said, tears beginning to run down her face.

That's when Mitch had done something he *never* should have done. He'd taken her into his arms. She'd laid her head on his shoulder, crying. And he'd felt desire that had no place in that room.

Mitch had met Troy—at that time Troy and Lily had been engaged—when the Family Tree staff had planned a dinner to welcome Mitch into the practice. Since he'd once served in the Army National Guard and Troy still had, they'd developed an immediate rapport, becoming friends. After Troy and Lily married, Troy had even asked Mitch to watch over Lily while he'd served overseas.

But then Troy had been killed in action, leaving Lily pregnant and alone.

When Lily had finally looked up at him, Mitch hadn't been sure *what* he'd seen there. Yet he'd known damn well it hadn't been interest. Gratitude, maybe?

She'd pulled away, wiped her eyes and mumbled an awkward apology, and they'd gone their separate ways. They'd gone back to being colleagues. She hadn't really confided in him again.

That was okay. Being merely colleagues was safer for both of them.

Now, however, it was the last week in February and

she was in labor. When he'd seen her double over on that dais, he'd felt panic twist his gut.

"Mitch!" A male voice called his name.

When he opened his eyes, he saw Jared, gesturing from the hall.

He stood immediately. "What's going on?"

"She wants you."

"What do you mean, she wants me?"

"She's in labor, and she wants you to coach her."

Her friends all glanced his way. He knew they were wondering why and so was he. But he wasn't going to ask Jared his questions. He was going to ask Lily.

"Suit up," Jared advised him. "When you're ready, she's in delivery room two."

Five minutes later, Mitch had pulled sterile garb over his clothes. It would feel strange being back in an operating-room setting, even though he had to admit a delivery room wasn't *exactly* that. When he'd rushed through the ER with Lily, one of the nurses had waved at him. Years ago, she'd worked with him in trauma surgery.

Sometimes he itched to be doing that kind of work again. Reflexively, he bent his fingers, most of them not responding well. But he'd gotten used to limited use of his right hand, as well as insomnia and nightmares. At least the stiffness in his shoulder and leg could be relieved with the right amount of exercise. He was damn lucky he'd left Iraq with his life. There was no point in complaining about what might have been. Changing his specialty to endocrinology had saved his sanity.

When he pushed open the door of the delivery room, he forgot about whether he should or shouldn't be there. Seeing Lily on the table, her face flushed, her hands clenched tight on the sheet, a protective urge took over. She was hooked up to monitors that measured the frequency and intensity of contractions as well as the babies' heart rates. She looked small and frightened...and fragile. Yet he knew she was the strongest woman he'd ever known. She'd proved that since her husband had died.

He strode to the bed, hooked a stool with his foot and positioned it beside her. Glancing at Emily Madison, Jared's wife and a professional midwife, he asked, "Don't you want Emily to coach you?"

Lily pushed damp hair behind her ear. "She's assisting Jared."

He knew why he was fighting being here. Witnessing a woman in labor, watching a birth, was an intimate experience. Right now, bonding with Lily would be foolish.

He could see a contraction gearing up in intensity. Maybe she just wanted him here instead of one of her friends because he might be more detached yet professional about the births.

With a mental kick that he hoped would push him toward that detachment, he took hold of her hand, felt the softness and warmth of it.

Suddenly she squeezed his fingers so hard he lost any feeling he *did* have left. But the pressure reminded him he had a job to do. If he concentrated on coaching, maybe he wouldn't notice how her chin quivered or how her eyes grew shiny with emotion.

When the contraction eased, he admitted, "I'm not sure how best to help you."

"You worked with men in the field. You helped

them. Help me the same way. Just help me *focus* on something."

She was right. He had helped men before and after surgeries, with mortar blasts exploding, with rocket-propelled grenades shattering the air. Finally he really did understand why she wanted him here.

Realizing what he had to do, he smoothed his thumb over the top of her hand, telling himself his need to touch her was simply for her comfort. "Watch my nose," Mitch ordered Lily.

She looked at him as if he was crazy. "You're kidding, right?"

"I'm not. Use it as your focal point and listen to the sound of my voice."

She focused on his eyes instead of his nose. He saw so many emotions there—worry, hope and grief…the resoluteness he'd admired as she'd exhibited it each day, ready to go on with her life and care for her twins.

Mitch saw her tense and turned to the monitor. With another contraction coming, he squeezed her hand. "You can do this."

She was still looking into his eyes instead of at his nose. He felt as if his heart was going to jump out of his chest. He felt as if…he *shouldn't* be here. Again, he warned himself that he couldn't make such an intimate connection. He should just be watching over her.

But how could he watch over her without getting involved?

At this moment, he wished he'd never made that promise to Troy.

At the foot of the bed, Emily said, "Lily, you can start pushing now."

At that moment, neonatologist Francesca Fitzgerald came into the room with two nurses behind her.

Lily gasped, "Francesca."

The doctor patted Lily's arm and summed up the situation with a quick assessment. "My team's here. You do your part and we'll take care of the rest."

Lily's contraction peaked and her cry of pain sliced through Mitch.

Jared encouraged her. "Good one, Lily. Come on. I want this baby out."

"You can do this," Mitch reminded her. He held her hand as the tension built in her body again. Her face reddened and she gave another fantastically effort-filled push.

All at once he heard Jared say, "I've got one!"

"Is she all right?" Lily asked. "Please tell me she's all right."

A light infant cry came from the area where Francesca was standing. It was very soft, but it *was* a cry.

"She's a beauty," Jared told her. "We might have a few minutes now. I want to get her sister out, as quickly as I can."

"I don't think I have a few minutes," Lily gasped. "It's starting again." She practically sat up with the strength and pain of the contraction.

"Use it," Mitch said. "Go with it."

"Just one more push," Emily encouraged her. "She's your youngest. You're going to have to coax her a little harder."

Mitch realized Lily wasn't focusing on him anymore. She was breathing when she had to, breathing any way she could. She needed a different type of support, physical as well as emotional. Knowing exactly what he had to do, Mitch stood, went to the head of the birthing table and wrapped his arm around her shoulders. He warned himself he was only a substitute for Troy. But he didn't feel like a substitute. His arms around Lily, he knew he was doing this for himself as well as his friend.

Tears swept down her cheeks. Her bangs were plastered to her forehead. She pushed her shoulder-length hair away from her face and stared straight ahead.

As her contraction built, her body curved into it, curved around it. Mitch held her as she delivered a second little girl.

Jared announced, "And here's princess number two."

Again he passed the infant to Francesca who worked at clearing her airway, cleaning her eyes, checking her lungs, hooking her up to the ventilator to help her breathe. When Mitch saw that, a lump rose in his throat.

"I've got them," Francesca reassured Lily. "I'll be around to give you a report as soon as I can." Then she pushed the babies away, out another door before Lily even glimpsed them.

Reluctantly, Mitch released Lily as she collapsed onto the bed, murmuring, "Maybe I should have quit work sooner and stayed in bed. It's often recommended with twins. But I rested the past two weeks. I kept my feet up as much as I could."

Mitch knew he had to keep Lily calm after her ordeal. "You did everything you thought was best. That's all you could do."

Lily surprised him when she caught his hand again and held it tight. "Troy should have been here. He should have seen his girls born. He should have helped me name them. He should have…he should have…"

"He should have never died," Mitch filled in.

Lily bowed her head and finally let the tears fall unchecked. Mitch did the only thing he could—he held her in his arms until she simply couldn't cry anymore.

Lily had been settled in her hospital room for at least two hours and was growing anxious. Why hadn't Francesca come yet? Wouldn't they have told her if something had happened to either of the babies?

Her gaze landed on Mitch, who was standing at the window. He was as calm as she was agitated. Where did that calm come from after what he'd been through? He'd been presented a Combat Medical Badge, awarded a Silver Star and a Purple Heart, though he never spoke of them. All Troy had told her was that Mitch had been involved in an IED explosion.

"How do you do it?" she asked, following the train of thoughts in her head.

Minus his jacket and tie, his tuxedo shirt was rumpled. He turned to look at her. "Do what?"

"Stay calm under any circumstances."

He shot her a wry half smile. "It's a learned technique."

Interested in anything that would keep her mind off what was going on down the hall, she asked, "Like meditation?"

Even though she'd worked with Mitch for more than two and a half years, she didn't know much about him. Just the little Troy had told her. She knew he was forty-five, had been born in Sagebrush—the small town where they both lived about fifteen minutes outside

Lubbock—but he had no family there. He'd been deployed to Iraq, injured and changed specialties—from trauma surgery to endocrinology—because he'd lost the fine motor coordination in his hand that he needed to perform surgery. But that was about the extent of her knowledge of his background.

"I learned several techniques," he replied, running his hand through his jet-black hair. "Meditation was one. Guided imagery was another."

Her gaze went to his hand and the ragged scars there. She wanted to ask if he'd learned the techniques when he'd been hurt. Had they been his method of recovering? But that was such personal territory. If he didn't mention Iraq himself, she knew better than to jump into it.

In spite of herself, she still remembered gazing into his eyes rather than looking at his nose while he'd coached her. Every time since the day she'd told him she was having twins, she'd felt such an intense...

She wasn't sure what it was she felt. Mitch knew things. He'd *felt* things. She could just instinctively sense that. The compassion he showed her seemed personal, but maybe he was that way with everyone.

"You know, your friends wanted to stay," he said.

Yes, they did. But they all had children and husbands and practices to see to. "I told them there was nothing they could do here. I'm going to call them as soon as we find out about the babies. Oh, Mitch, what's taking so long?"

Leaving his pensive position at the window, he crossed to her bed. He was so tall...confident...strong.

She remembered being held in his arms—in the exam room at the practice, on the dais, in the delivery room. His cologne had wrapped around her as he'd given her his strength. That's why she'd needed him with her through the delivery—because he was so strong. Now when she looked at him she could hardly swallow.

With one push of his booted foot, the comfortable chair by the nightstand now sat beside her bed. He sank down into the chair. It was well after 1:00 a.m. and she knew he had to be tired after a full day of work. She should tell him to go home, too. But he seemed willing to see her through this and she felt she needed him here.

Though she realized her body was ready for a good long rest, she couldn't relax. Adrenaline was still rushing through her because she was so concerned about her twins.

In the labor room, Mitch had taken her hand. Now he didn't.

Why should it matter? she wondered. She quickly decided it didn't. After all, she was still in love with Troy. At times, she thought she heard him in the next room. Other times, she expected his booming voice to announce that he was home. She fought back sudden emotion.

Mitch's deep, even voice reassured her. "I have a feeling Francesca will only come to you after the babies are stabilized...after she can tell you something for certain."

"You're so honest," Lily blurted out. "I wanted you to say she probably had another emergency and that's why it was taking her so long."

"Do you believe that?"

His expression wasn't stern. His lean cheeks and high cheekbones just made him appear that way sometimes.

As his black brows drew together just a little, he looked expectant…as if he knew she couldn't lie to herself.

"It's possible," she murmured.

"Yes, it's possible," he agreed.

"Talk to me about something," she pleaded. "Anything."

She knew she might be asking for a lot. Mitch communicated, but only when he had something to say. Chitchat didn't seem to be in his nature. But now she would be glad for anything her mind could latch on to.

"When is Raina McGraw's baby due?"

Lily smiled, picturing her friend with her rounding stomach. "June fifth. Talk about having a lot on your plate."

"I understand Shep adopted three children before she married him."

"They're still in the process with Manuel, their two-and-a-half-year-old. Shep had started adoption proceedings, but then he and Raina married. It was almost like starting over. Their housekeeper, Eva, is wonderful, but Raina could be running from morning to night once the baby's born. I think she's going to take a leave from her practice."

"Have you decided yet how long you're going to stay out?"

"I'll make up my mind soon. Everything about my life is in flux right now."

"You don't have to decide right away. You might have to consider getting help with the twins."

"No, I won't need it. My roommate Angie—Gina's sister—says she'll help me. She's a nurse, away right now on the disaster relief team. But she should be back soon. Besides, there are lots of moms who take care of two babies."

"Not necessarily at the same time." His tone held a warning note that maybe she was being a little too Pollyanna-ish.

"I can handle it, Mitch. You'll see."

She was contemplating the idea of breast-feeding both babies when the door pushed open and Francesca walked in. She seemed surprised to see Mitch there, but didn't comment.

Lily hadn't known Francesca very long. But one evening, the women who'd lived in the Victorian house on a quiet street in Sagebrush had gathered there and just enjoyed a ladies' night of chatting and sharing backgrounds. All of them were connected in so many ways—through their professions, friendships or family ties.

Lily had felt so alone after Troy had died, but that night all of the women had made her feel as if she had a support network.

"Tell me," Lily said to Francesca.

"Your older daughter weighs four point two pounds, is seventeen inches long, and needs a little time to put on weight. We're giving her CPAP treatment. She's breathing on her own and is definitely a crier when she's unhappy."

The continuous positive airway pressure would help the infant breathe but not breathe for her. Lily's heart swelled with love for this tiny baby although she hadn't even laid eyes on her yet. "And my youngest?" Lily's voice shook a little bit when she asked.

"She weighs four pounds, is sixteen and a half inches and had trouble breathing." Francesca immediately held up both hands. "Now, don't panic. We have her stabilized. She's on a ventilator for now—"

"Oh my God!" Lily's chest felt so tight she could hardly breathe.

"I mean it, Lily. Don't panic. We'll wean her off it. Her lungs need to develop and, of course, she needs to gain weight, too, before she can go home."

"When can I see them?"

Francesca sighed. "I shouldn't allow it, but I know you're not going to rest or get any sleep until I let you visit them."

Lily nodded. She was happy, afraid and plain exhausted. But she had to see them.

"All right. I'll find a wheelchair. But you can only have a few minutes with them, and then I need to tuck you in. Childbirth is natural, but it's traumatic, too, and you need time to recover."

"I know," Lily said. "When do you think I'll be discharged?"

"You'll have to ask Jared that, but my guess is you'll be here until Sunday morning."

At least she'd be here so she could visit her babies. *Her babies.* Everything about their birth came rushing back, especially Mitch's presence and support. "Can Mitch come, too?"

Francesca hesitated and looked from one of them to the other. "This is just for a few minutes. You both have to wear masks and sterile gowns. I'll be right back."

Mitch looked troubled. "Are you sure you want me there, Lily?"

"You helped me bring them into the world. Of course, I want you there."

Maybe it was because of the letter Troy had left for

her. In it, he'd told her he'd asked Mitch to look after her
if anything happened to him. He'd trusted Mitch, and
that made it easy for her to trust him, too. He'd certainly
come through for her tonight.

Ten minutes later, Lily and Mitch were in the NIC
unit, staring at her two precious little girls. The babies
absolutely snatched Lily's breath away.

Mitch stood behind her, his hand on her shoulder.
"Have you considered names?"

"Now that I see them, I can name them." She pointed
to her firstborn, saying lightly, "Sophie, I'd like you to
meet Mitch. He helped me bring you into this world."

Her baby opened her eyes, seemed to gaze at them
both for a few seconds before she closed them again.

Lily's heart overflowed with love as her focus turned
to her youngest, who needed help to breathe.

Mitch's fingers tightened on Lily's shoulder and
she was so grateful for his quiet strength, his stalwart
caring.

"And this tiny angel is—" Lily's voice caught. Finally
she managed to say, "Her name is Grace."

Mitch crouched down beside Lily so he could see her
children from her vantage point. The slant of his jaw
almost grazed her cheek as he reassured her, "They're
going to gain weight and strength each day."

When Mitch turned to her instead of the twins, Lily's
heart beat faster. "Thank you," she said simply.

"You're welcome," Mitch returned with a crooked
smile. Just for tonight she'd let Mitch Cortega be her
rock. Just for tonight, she'd depend on him.

Then she'd stand on her own two feet and raise her
babies alone.

Chapter Two

Mitch stood in Lily's hospital room on Sunday afternoon. She was ready to go home and be a mom, but her babies couldn't go home with her. At least, not for a few weeks, and only then if no further problems developed. She didn't want to leave them, but she had no choice. She also couldn't drive herself home. Gina was in Houston again. Angie was still away, helping flood victims. And Raina, six months pregnant with a new husband and three boys to think about, had enough on her plate.

So Mitch had offered to drive Lily home, and she'd accepted. In fact, the thought of being with him again had made her feel…less worried. But now that he was standing in the room, dressed in jeans and a dark-green V-neck sweater, her pulse was speeding faster. She told herself she was just excited about leaving the hospital.

However, she snuck another peek at him and felt her stomach flutter.

Maybe she should have just paid taxi fare from Lubbock to Sagebrush instead of accepting his assistance so readily.

He seemed to read some of her thoughts. "I know you want to be independent, Lily, but I'm only giving you a ride home. You'll be driving again soon."

She did have to put this in perspective. "I just never expected to be going home without my babies and without—" She abruptly stopped.

"And without Troy," he filled in, not afraid to say it.

Blinking very fast she zipped the overnight case that Raina had dropped off for her. "I'm ready to get out of here and finish decorating the nursery. Everything needs to be perfect when my girls come home."

Mitch came up behind her, gently took her by the shoulders and turned her around. "You don't have to hide what you're feeling."

"I have to get *over* what I'm feeling, Mitch. I have two babies to take care of, to support. I can't think about Troy not being here and do what I have to do."

"You can't deny it, either. That will only bring you more heartache in the end."

Gazing into his deep brown eyes, she felt that unsettled sensation in the pit of her stomach again.

"I'm ready to go," she said firmly. She'd cry at night when she was too tired to do anything else. In the meantime, she was going to put a life together for her children.

Mitch dropped his hands from her shoulders and

picked up her overnight case. "Then let's get you home."

Their fifteen-minute drive from Lubbock to the small Texas town of Sagebrush was quiet for the most part. Mitch didn't seem to feel the need to talk and stared straight ahead as he drove. She had too many thoughts buzzing through her mind to want to be involved in conversation—including her unsettling awareness of the black-haired, broad-shouldered, protective man sitting beside her. Before her labor, hadn't she looked at Mitch as the person he was? Had she just seen him merely as a colleague? Simply a friend of Troy's? A person on the outskirts of her life but not really *in* her life?

He pulled into the driveway in front of the detached garage at the large blue Victorian-style house with yellow shutters, then turned to her with questions in his eyes, voicing one of them. "Who's going to be staying with you?"

"No one's staying with me."

Silence fell over the SUV as wind buffeted it.

"Isn't Angie back yet?" Mitch asked.

"No. When she's called away on the disaster relief team, there's no knowing how long she'll be gone."

"What about Raina?"

"I can't expect her to come over here and sit with me with all her responsibilities. Besides, I don't need a babysitter."

"As soon as you walk into that house, you're going to be surprised by how tired you feel. You can't stay here alone tonight."

Lily suddenly felt panicked without knowing exactly why. "What are you suggesting?"

"I'm not suggesting anything. I'm going to give you

two options. One, I can take you home with me and you can stay there for the night."

She was shaking her head already.

"Or, two, I can sleep on your couch."

She was still shaking her head.

"Is your refrigerator stocked?"

"I don't know."

"Do you feel like cooking supper?"

Though she didn't want to admit it, she did feel really tired. "I can make myself an egg."

"I seem to remember Jared ordering you to go home and rest today, for what's left of it, and turn in early tonight."

"He's just being cautious."

Mitch unbuckled his seat belt and shifted behind the wheel to face her. "I know as doctors we make the worst patients, but you've got to be sensible. When those babies come home in a few weeks, you have to be ready *physically* as well as emotionally. So, at least for today, accept help without argument."

Was she being unreasonable? *Was* she trying to be too strong? Why was that? Because she didn't want anyone helping her...or she suddenly didn't want *Mitch* helping her? The thought of him sleeping on her couch tonight made her stomach do something more than flutter. She felt as if she'd gone over the top of a Ferris wheel.

But she certainly wasn't going to Mitch's place. The gossips in Sagebrush would have a field day.

"Let's go inside and you can curl up on the sofa," he suggested. "I'll get you something to drink and we'll go from there."

"Don't you have other things to do today?"

"Repairing winter's damage to the patio? Sweeping out my garage?" He gave her one of his rare smiles.

Ever since Mitch had started with the practice, she'd noticed the long hours he worked, longer than any of the other physicians. He even scheduled consultations on Saturdays. He had rarely taken off work in the time she'd known him. Didn't he have a life outside of the fertility lab? Did he have friends other than the service buddies Troy had once mentioned? Mitch was an enigma, a puzzle she couldn't solve—one she shouldn't be interested in at all.

She nibbled on her lower lip for a couple of seconds and then asked, "Do you know how to cook?"

When he chuckled, she liked the sound of it. "I do. My mother taught me the basics," he said with fond remembrance. "I do all right."

The air in his SUV seemed stifling. She was relieved they were separated in the bucket seats because being physically close to Mitch now seemed…dangerous.

She asked in a low voice, "Why are you doing this, Mitch?"

"I made a promise to Troy. I keep my promises."

That's what she thought. This was duty for Mitch. He was a man who knew duty and honor well.

She let out a long breath. "All right, you can sleep on my couch. But just tonight. That's it. Tomorrow I'm on my own again."

"Deal," he agreed.

Even though he said it, she saw a considering flicker in his eyes. How long would his promise to Troy hold?

Minutes later they were escaping the blustery weather outside and walking into the old house that Lily now thought of as home. Last September she'd moved out of the apartment she'd shared with Troy because the memories there had been too painful.

She breathed in the scent of cinnamon emanating from the potpourri dish beside the Tiffany lamp in the foyer. Angie had filled it before Christmas. Her housemate had understood how difficult the holidays would be for Lily and had included her in her family's celebrations. So had Gina and, of course, Raina. They'd kept Lily too busy to think if not feel. At night, alone in her room, she'd faced her loss and spoken to her unborn babies about their dad and about what their first Christmas the following year might bring. She had to look toward the future.

"Where would you like your overnight case?" Mitch asked, stepping in behind her.

"Upstairs on my bed would be great."

"The steps won't be a problem?"

"Not at all. But I'll only do them once today."

"Which room is yours?"

A jolt of reality hit when she realized Mitch would be standing in her bedroom in a few minutes. He'd see the baby catalogs and magazines splayed across the chest at the foot of the bed, as well as the photo of Troy on her dresser. What else would he notice?

And why was the idea of Mitch standing in her bedroom so unnerving?

"What's wrong?" he asked.

"Nothing. My bedroom's the second one on the right. It's the one with the yellow rose wallpaper."

"Got it," he said with the flash of a smile that made her breath hitch a little.

Confused, she decided she was just tired from the trip

home and worried about her babies. She wasn't reacting to Mitch as a man. She absolutely wasn't.

When Mitch returned downstairs, she was pulling greens and carrots from the refrigerator.

He came up beside her and took them out of her hands. "Stop. Today you're not doing a thing. Wouldn't you be more comfortable in the living room in an easy chair?"

He was a doctor, too. He knew what her body had been through, though she was trying to deny it.

"Don't you have a good book you want to read?" he teased.

She supposed humor was better than anything else. Maybe it would make this jumpy feeling she had when she was around him go away. "I'm sure I can find something to read."

When she took a last glance around, he said, "Relax and trust me."

Trust him. That was the tall and short of it. She did. And trusting him formed a bond that she just didn't want right now. She'd trusted Troy because he was her husband. But now he was gone, and she shouldn't be able to simply turn around and trust another man so easily.

Should she?

"What's going on in your head?" Mitch asked with gentle persuasion.

Nothing he'd want to know about. Her doubts and questions and issues were all hers. None of it had anything to do with him. "I'm just...wired and tired at the same time."

He set the greens and carrots on the counter. Then he nudged her around and walked her toward the living room. He was a good six inches taller than she was and she felt petite beside him.

The heat of his palm on her shoulder seeped through her knit top. She should have worn a sweater. This old house could be drafty. If she'd worn a sweater, she wouldn't feel the warmth of his hand at all...or remember him holding hers as Sophie was born.

He released her as they reached the sofa. Then he stood there and waited and she realized he wanted her to sit. He definitely was a commanding male. Why would that change simply because he was trying to be her friend? Men in the military had a particular bearing, a straightness of their backs, a tautness of their shoulders, that made them seem *more* than ordinary men. Not that anything about Mitch today seemed military. His jeans, sweater and even his leather boots looked comfortable. She couldn't remember ever seeing him dressed so casually before.

She sank down onto the sofa.

"Put your legs up," he ordered.

She didn't usually take orders well. "I'll be bored," she muttered.

While he pulled the afghan from the back of the sofa and spread it over her, he asked, "Don't you knit or something?"

"Crochet," she corrected automatically, then pointed to the tapestry bag beside the easy chair. She knew if she made a move to get it, he wouldn't let her.

When he stooped to pick up the bag, she noticed the play of his shoulder muscles, the length of his upper torso, his slim hips. A tingle that she relegated to post-birth pangs rippled through her belly. Looking away, she pulled the afghan up higher.

He brought the bag to her and settled it in her lap. "What are you making?"

After opening the Velcro closure, she extracted a pink sweater that sported one sleeve. "I didn't know whether to make these both pink or not. You know, stereotypes and all. But then I thought, two baby girls. What could be cuter than matching pink sweaters?"

He laughed. "I'm sure Sophie and Grace will agree."

She turned the sweater over in her hands and then admitted, "I was an only child. I wanted a sister desperately. Sophie and Grace will always have each other." She looked up at him again. "Do you have brothers or sisters?" She really didn't know anything about Mitch's background or his childhood.

"Nope. No brothers or sisters."

"Troy and his sister Ellie were close," Lily said in a low voice.

"He talked about her often," Mitch responded, in the way he had ever since Troy had been killed. She was grateful he made it all right for her to speak about her husband and anything connected to him.

"She's in a tough situation right now," Lily said to Mitch. "She had a small store where she sold her own line of baby clothes. But her area of Oklahoma was hard hit by the economic downturn and she had to close the store."

"What's she doing now?"

"She's trying to take her business to the internet."

"Is she coming for a visit?"

"Ellie and Troy's mom, Darlene, both want to visit after the babies come home." She'd always gotten along well with Ellie and Darlene...with all of Troy's family.

She knew he'd moved to Texas because the construction market had been thriving around Lubbock, unlike Oklahoma. She'd often wished his family wasn't so far away.

An odd expression crossed Mitch's face, one she couldn't decipher. He said, "You'll have a lot of people to help with the babies. That's just what you need."

"*Is* that what I need, Mitch? I'm their mom. I want to take care of them myself."

"Sure you do. But twins are a lot of work. There was a kid in my neighborhood when I was growing up. His mother had twins. She was always run ragged. And when you go back to work, you're definitely going to need child care."

"I have to go back," she said. "Insurance money and savings will only go so far."

"You'll have Troy's benefits," Mitch reminded her.

"That money is going into a trust fund for the twins."

He didn't contradict her, or try to convince her otherwise. She wanted to give her girls the advantages she'd had growing up. Yet, most of all, she wanted them to appreciate the people around them who loved them. When she'd lost her parents, she'd realized how little material possessions actually meant, and she'd grown up quickly.

"Did you grow up here in Sagebrush?" she asked Mitch, curious about his childhood.

"Yes, I did."

Frustrated he wasn't more expansive, she prompted, "But you don't have family here."

"No, I don't."

"Mitch," she said, letting her frustration show.

"What do you want to know, Lily? Just ask."

Studying his collar-length black hair, his chiseled features, she let the question pop into her head. *Are you just here out of duty or do you care?* Instead she replied, "I *am* asking. But you're not telling me much."

"And why is this suddenly important?"

That was a good question. "I'm not sure. I guess talking about Ellie, thinking about how I'm going to raise the twins— It just made me wonder, that's all. At least give me something to think about while I rest and twiddle my thumbs."

"Crochet," he pointed out.

"Same difference."

The silence in the living room enveloped them for a few moments until Mitch said, "Your background and mine are very different."

"How do you know about mine?"

"Troy shared some of it when we played pool."

Lily's husband and Mitch had gone out and shared an evening of guy stuff now and then, the same way she shared time with her friends.

"Just what did he tell you?"

Mitch's shrug told her he was attempting to make the conversation casual. "That your father was a respected scientist and professor at Stanford. That your mother was a pharmacist who developed her own line of cosmetics and did quite well with them. Something about after your father died, she sold the formula to provide you with a college education."

"Yes, she did," Lily murmured, mind-traveling back to a time that was filled with bittersweet memories. "Daddy died of a massive coronary when I was in high school. My mom died of breast cancer when I was in college. Losing them both made me want to find a profession that gave life."

"If your father taught at Stanford, how did you end up *here?*"

"My mom had a friend who lived in Lubbock, so we moved here. But she and my dad had always planned I'd go to their alma mater. I was at Stanford when she got sick. I flew home as often as I could, but then took off a semester when we called in hospice."

"You've had a lot of loss."

"The people I love leave me." She stared at her hands when she said it, but then she raised her gaze to his. "I know. I know. I shouldn't believe that. If nothing else, I should think positive to change the pattern. But this negative pattern is awfully fresh again and it's hard not to wonder."

"You have two little girls now to love."

"I do. And you can bet, I *will* be an overprotective mom."

"I don't think there's anything wrong with that."

Somehow the conversation had rolled back to Lily again. Mitch was so good at deflecting. Why had she never realized that? But she was also determined to delve below the surface.

Hiking herself up higher against the sofa arm, she nodded toward the space at the end of the couch where her feet had been. "Tell me how you grew up."

He looked as reluctant to sit on her couch as she was to have him sleep there tonight. But in the end, he decided she wouldn't rest until he gave her something. So he sat on the sofa, his thigh brushing one of her stockinged feet. He looked terrifically uncomfortable. "There's not much to it."

She waited, her gaze on his rugged profile.

With a grimace, he finally said, "My father married my mother because she was pregnant when they were both eighteen."

She knew Mitch was probably going to need some prompting, so she asked, "Did it last?"

Mitch's brows drew together as he, obviously reluctant, answered, "He stuck around for a year, then took off on his motorcycle and bailed. She went to business school and became a medical transcriber, but she couldn't always find work. Other times she held two jobs, cleaned offices at night and saved for when times were thin again. I was determined to make life better for both of us."

"Did you always want to be a doctor?"

"Do you mean was it a lifelong wish from childhood? No. Actually, at first I thought I might become a stockbroker or an investment banker."

Lily couldn't help but smile. She couldn't imagine Mitch as either of those. She didn't know why. She just couldn't. "So why aren't you working on Wall Street?"

"I was good at sports...basketball. I won a scholarship to college. But during my sophomore year my mother got sick and didn't tell me. She didn't have insurance so she didn't go to the doctor. She developed pneumonia and died."

"Oh, Mitch. I'm sorry. That had to be awful for you."

Again he looked uncomfortable revealing this part of his past. "She'd been my motivator. After she died, I took a nosedive. I'd been a good student, but my grades tanked. Then one day, after a few months of drinking into the night and sleeping too late to get up for class, I looked out the dorm window and knew that campus wasn't *real* life. Guys hooking up with girls, frat parties, learning to play teachers for better grades. I thought about my mom's life, how hard it had been and how it ended, and I decided to make a difference. I wanted to help patients who didn't have much of a chance. I wanted to give life when it was hardly there any longer. So I juggled two jobs, got my B.S., and went on to med school. I decided on trauma surgery. In my last year of residency, September 11th happened."

Lily thought of Raina and her first husband, a firefighter, who had lost his life that day. Her knowledge of Mitch's character and her intuition where he was concerned urged her to ask, "And that's when you signed up for the Army National Guard?"

"Yes."

"When did you go to Iraq?"

"Two years later."

They were both quiet for a few moments.

Mitch flexed his hand and moved his fingers as she often saw him do, and she knew he was remembering something he never talked about…something that caused those deep fatigue lines around his eyes some mornings.

To break the heavy silence, she asked, "Are you happy being part of our fertility practice?" She and two other doctors had been in unanimous agreement, voting him into their partnership.

"You mean would I rather be performing surgery? Sure. But I like what I do. You and me, Jon and Hillary…we give the seeds of life a chance, as well as at-risk pregnancies. That's rewarding. What I miss is not being part of the Guard, no longer having that unique camaraderie and sense of spirit. Before deployment, it was tough trying to be a doctor as well as a guardsman. But it was what I wanted to be doing."

Abruptly he stood, his body language telling her that this conversation was over. He already knew Lily was the type who wanted to know more, who would ask questions until she got her answers. He was cutting that off before it could go any further. To her surprise, she already missed his presence at the end of the sofa.

"I checked your refrigerator and you have a couple of choices," he said with a forced smile. "Scrambled eggs, scrambled eggs with asparagus and bacon on the side, or... I think I saw sausage in there that I could turn into sausage and pasta of some kind, maybe with canned tomatoes."

"Are you kidding me?" Her eyes were open wide and she was staring at him as if she really didn't know him.

"I told you my mom taught me the basics. But in college I had an apartment with two other guys. I couldn't stomach pizza every night, so I cooked. I borrowed a cookbook or two from the library and they kept me going for the year."

"You're just full of surprises," Lily said, laying her head back against the arm of the sofa, suddenly tired and feeling weak.

"Is the adrenaline finally giving out?" he asked her.

"If you mean do I feel like a wet noodle, yes. Are you happy now?"

The corner of his mouth turned down. "Seeing you tired doesn't make me happy. But knowing that because of it you'll get some rest does." He took hold of the afghan and pulled it above her breasts. He made sure she was covered from there to her toes. Then he gave it a little tuck under her hip so it wouldn't fall away.

Mitch's fingers were strong and long. She felt heat from them with just that quick touch. He'd used his left hand. From what she'd heard, he didn't have much feeling in the fingers of his right hand.

She caught his arm before he moved away.

His gaze crashed into hers and they stared at each other for a few moments.

"Thank you for bringing me home."

"No problem," he responded, as if it was no big deal.

But it was a big deal to Lily. She'd never forget his friendship with Troy. She'd certainly never forget his kindness to her. But something about that kindness and her acceptance of it unsettled her. She had to figure out why it bothered her so much that Mitch would be sleeping on her couch tonight.

Chapter Three

Lily stared at the TV that evening, not really focused on the newsmagazine show that was airing. She was too aware of Mitch rattling the back screen door, fixing loose weather stripping.

Over supper they'd talked about the house and former tenants, needing dispassionate conversation. When they didn't stay on neutral territory, they seemed to wander into intensity…or awkwardness that came from being alone together. It was odd, really. For the past two and a half years while working with Mitch, she'd found him easy to be with. Now…

The phone rang and Lily picked up the cordless from the end table. When she saw Gina's number on caller ID, she breathed a sigh of relief.

"Hi," Gina said. "How are you and Sophie and Grace?"

"I called the hospital a little bit ago. They're doing okay. And I'm…good. I'm at home."

"So you said in your message. I'm sorry I just got it. My plane had a delay taking off. It was a whirlwind trip, leaving yesterday and coming back today. But I didn't want to be away from Daniel and Logan any longer than I had to be."

A baby development expert, Gina had received an offer from a Houston hospital to start her Baby Grows center there, too. Lily was sure Gina would someday not only have an additional Baby Grows center in Houston but many all around the country.

"So Mitch is keeping you company? How's that going?"

"It's okay. It's just…he's hovering. He insists I shouldn't be alone today. He gave me the option to sleep over at his place, or his sleeping on my couch. So he's sleeping here on my couch tonight."

"Are you okay with that?"

"Sure." But Lily knew her voice didn't sound sure. A man who wasn't her husband sleeping under her roof. Is that what was bothering her? Or was there more to it?

"Do you want me to come over?"

"No," Lily was quick to answer. "You need to be with your family."

"I was going to take off work tomorrow. Why don't I drive over first thing? Then Mitch can go to Family Tree."

"Are you sure you don't have other things you have to do?"

"I don't," Gina replied. "Tomorrow we can talk about Sophie and Grace, possibly visit them, and maybe I can get some things ready for you."

Seeing her twins. Baby talk. Girl talk. That sounded great to Lily. "I really appreciate this."

"No problem. Have you heard from Angie?"

Angie was Gina's sister, and Lily knew Gina worried about her when she worked on the team. "No. Have you?"

"No, not since she reached the Gulf. But the disaster relief team really doesn't have time for anything but helping the victims." After a short pause, she asked, "Why don't I stop at the bakery and pick up croissants on my way over?"

"I'm supposed to be losing weight, not gaining it."

"You don't have that much to lose. Besides, if you're going to pump milk and then breast-feed, you need some extra calories."

"The croissants sound good. That way I can convince Mitch he doesn't have to make breakfast."

"Did he make supper?"

"He did. And now he's doing some minor repairs on the house."

It must have been her tone of voice when she said it that made Gina ask, "That bothers you?"

"I don't want to be indebted to him. Do you know what I mean?"

"Oh, I know. But remember, Troy asked him to watch over you. That's what he's doing."

Last fall, Lily had shared Troy's letter with Gina, Angie and Raina. They also knew Mitch was simply fulfilling a promise. She should be grateful instead of uncomfortable.

Lily had just ended the call when Mitch strode into the living room. She told him, "Gina's coming over early tomorrow morning so you don't have to worry about me."

No change of expression crossed Mitch's face, but there was a flicker of reaction in his eyes that said he would worry anyway.

"I have a new client tomorrow who will be making decisions about in vitro fertilization and a few follow-up appointments after that. So if you need anything, I can try to rearrange my schedule."

She jumped in. "No need. I'll be sorting baby clothes with Gina and hanging decorations on the nursery walls. I wasn't prepared for an early delivery, which isn't like me at all!"

Mitch set the duct tape he'd carried in on an end table. "You wanted to stay in the pregnant zone as long as you could."

Although diplomatic, what he wasn't saying was obvious. She'd wanted to put off the idea of becoming a mother without Troy by her side for as long as possible. For once in her life, denial had definitely been more palatable than reality.

But now reality had smacked her in the face.

"You look lost," Mitch said, with a gentle edge to his voice.

That gentleness fell over her like a warm cloak. But then she had to ask herself, *did* she feel lost? Adrift? Alone? But she wasn't alone when she had good friends helping her. "No, not lost. Just off balance. I hate the unexpected. And my life has been one unexpected crisis after the other."

Rounding the coffee table, he approached her and she wished he'd sit beside her on the sofa. But he didn't.

"Sophie and Grace coming home will be grounding. You'll see."

His dark eyes didn't waver from hers and she felt sudden heat rising in her cheeks. Not from looking at Mitch! How many times had she looked at him in just that way?

No. Not just *this* way.

"The bedding for the sofa is upstairs," she said in a rush. "I'll get it."

"Are you staying up there?"

"I suppose." She produced a smile. "You'll have the downstairs to yourself if you want to watch TV or get a snack."

"I'll walk up with you."

There was no point in protesting. What would she do? Toss him the bedding over the banister?

When she swung her legs over the side of the sofa, Mitch was there, holding out his hand to help her up. She could be stubborn. Or she could accept a hand up when she needed it.

His strong fingers closed over hers, and her heart raced as her mind searched for something to say.

"Take it slowly," he reminded her as she rose to her feet.

Everything Mitch said today seemed to be full of deeper meaning. Although she longed to keep her hand in his, she slid it free and headed to the stairs.

A few minutes later in the hall on the second floor, Lily stopped by the linen closet and opened the door. Blankets lay folded on the shelf above her head. She reached up but she shouldn't have bothered. Mitch was there, behind her, easily pulling a blanket from the closet. His superior height and strength was obvious.

She could sense both, even though he wasn't touching her. Jittery, tired and anxious about what was going to happen next, she knew her hormones were out of whack. That was the best explanation she could think of to explain how she was feeling around Mitch.

He stepped away, bedding in hand. "This is great."

"Don't be silly. You need a sheet and pillow." And *she* needed something to do with her hands. She needed something to do with her mind. She needed something to *do*.

Choosing a pale blue sheet, she yanked a matching pillowcase from a stack. "The extra pillows are way up on the top shelf," she explained, moving away, letting him reach.

He easily removed one of those, too.

"I wish the sofa pulled out. You're going to be uncomfortable all scrunched up."

He laughed. "Believe me, I've slept on a lot worse. You worry too much, Lily. Did anyone ever tell you that?"

Her husband's name came to her lips, but she didn't say it. She didn't have to. Mitch knew.

He looked disconcerted for a second—just a second—but then he took the sheets from her arms. "Do you have a phone in your room?"

"My cell phone is in my purse. You brought that up with my suitcase. Why?"

"If you need something, call me. You might go to bed and an hour from now figure out you want a pack of crackers or a glass of milk."

There was only one way to answer with a man like Mitch. "I'll call you if I need you."

But somehow they both knew she wouldn't.

She went to the door to her room, which was only a few feet away. He didn't move until she stepped over the threshold and murmured, "Good night."

He gave her a slight nod, responded, "Good night, Lily," and headed for the stairs.

As she closed her door, she leaned against it and sighed. She wanted to make up the sofa for him so it would be comfortable.

How silly a notion was that?

"What do you mean you sent Gina home?" Mitch demanded as he stood in Lily's living room the following evening, a gift-wrapped box under one arm.

"She arrived before I was up this morning, as you know. She helped me ready the nursery. She took me to see the babies, and then I told her she should go home to her husband and son."

"And she just went?" He seemed astonished by that idea.

"She protested, but I plopped here on the sofa, told her I'd stay here, and she saw I meant it."

Lily was one exasperating woman! There was no doubt about that. But he had to admire her in spite of himself. "What did you do for dinner?"

"What is this, the third degree?"

He just arched a brow.

"Gina made a casserole for lunch and I had leftovers, with a salad and all that. What did *you* have?" she returned, almost cheekily.

All day he'd thought about eating dinner with her last night…saying good-night at the end of the day, spending the night on her couch in the strong grip of an insomnia he knew too well. Yet that was better than waking up in a sweat after too-real flashbacks or nightmares. Moments of sensual awareness when Lily had come downstairs this morning had been unsettling enough to push him on his way as soon as Gina had arrived.

Answering her, he said, "I went to the drive-through at my favorite burger joint." At her expression, he laughed. "Don't look so outraged. I have to do that once a week to keep fit."

Lily laughed then, even though she tried not to. That was the first real laugh he'd heard from her since before—even he had trouble saying it sometimes—since before Troy had died. He wanted to keep her spirits up. "So...how are Sophie and Grace?"

"Sit down," Lily said, motioning to the sofa. "I hate it when you loom. What's under your arm?"

"We'll get to that." He considered her comment. "And I don't loom."

"Whatever you say," she said too quickly, with a little smile.

Shaking his head, he set the box on the coffee table and lowered himself to the sofa. Not too close to her. Before he'd driven over here, he'd warned himself about that.

"The babies are so small," she explained, worried. "I can touch them but I can't hold them, and I'm dying to hold them."

"You'll soon be able to hold Sophie, if not Grace. How's their weight?" he asked, digging for the bottom line like a doctor.

"They're holding their own. My milk should be in soon and I'm going to pump it—" She stopped as her cheeks turned more pink.

"Don't be embarrassed. I'm a doctor, Lily. We talk

about this all the time with our patients." Right now he had to think of her as a patient so other images didn't trip over each other in his head.

"I know. But it seems different with...us."

Yes, something *did* seem different. Her perception of him? His of her? The fact that they'd been friends and maybe now something more was going on?

Nothing should be going on. It was way too soon for her. Maybe way too late for him.

"Can you tell them apart?" he asked, knowing conversation about her little girls would be comforting for her.

"Of course. Sophie's nose is turned up a little bit more at the end than Grace's. Grace's chin is just a little daintier, a tad more refined. They both have Troy's forehead and probably his eyes. It's a little too soon to tell. Sophie's a half inch longer than Grace, but Grace could catch up if she gains weight."

"She'll gain weight. They both will."

"Grace is still on the ventilator." Lily's voice trembled a bit.

Needing to fortify her with the truth, he asked, "What does Francesca say?"

"Francesca insists they're doing as well as can be expected and I have to give them time. I just feel like I should be doing something. Do you know what I mean?"

"Oh, yeah. Sitting still isn't easy for either one of us." He patted the box. "That's why I brought this along. Doing is always better than worrying."

"A gift?" Lily tore the wrapping paper off and read the information on the outside of the box. "Oh, Mitch, this is one of those new baby monitors."

"It is. The screen is small, but there's a portable handset you can carry with you to another room. So I'm also going to hook up a larger monitor you won't need binoculars to see. It's in my car."

"I can't let you—"

He shook his finger at her. "Don't even say it. You're going to be running yourself ragged when those babies come home. Having cameras in their cribs and a monitor down here so you can see them will help save a little bit of your energy."

"It will save a lot of my energy. Thank you."

Her blue eyes seemed to try to look inside him, into his heart...into his soul. That unsettled him. His soul was tormented at times by everything that had happened in Iraq. He hadn't been able to save his friend, and that, along with the PTSD symptoms, clawed at his heart. He quickly replied, "You're welcome. Why don't I get this hooked up? That way it will be ready whenever you bring the babies home."

"The cribs were delivered this morning. Gina supervised so I didn't have to run up and down the steps. But I don't know if she put the bedding on."

"Don't worry about it. I can position the cameras with the bedding on or off."

"Do you need my help? I can come up—"

"No." If Lily came upstairs, she would definitely be a distraction. "I brought along a toolbox and everything I might need. You drink a glass of milk and crochet or something."

"Drink a glass of milk?" She was smiling and her question was filled with amusement.

That smile of hers packed a wallop. It turned up the corners of her very pretty mouth. It seemed to make the few freckles across her cheeks more evident, her face actually glow.

Had he been attracted to Lily before Troy's death? If he was honest with himself, he had to say he had been. But attraction was one thing, acting on it was another. He'd shut it down when he'd learned she and Troy were to be married. He and Troy had become good friends and he'd congratulated them both at their wedding, always keeping his distance from Lily.

Being colleagues at their practice had been difficult at times. But not impossible. He kept their dealings strictly professional. They'd been cohorts, interacting on an intellectual level. He and Troy had been close. He and Lily? They'd just existed in the same universe.

Until...after Troy had died. When Mitch had hugged Lily that day after her ultrasound, he'd experienced desire and felt like an SOB because of it. That day, Mitch had realized that if he was going to keep his promise to Troy, he couldn't deny his attraction any longer. At least to himself. *She* didn't have to know about it.

But now—

Now nothing had changed. He had baggage. She had a world of grief and loss and new responsibility to deal with.

Turning away from her smile, which could affect him more than he wanted to admit, he muttered, "Milk's good for you and the babies. You've got to keep your vitamin D level up, along with your calcium. I'll go get what I need from the SUV and be right back."

Sometimes retreat was the best part of valor. Remembering that might save them both from an awkward or embarrassing situation.

* * *

Lily was emptying the dishwasher when Mitch called her into the living room. She'd been aware of his footfalls upstairs, the old floors creaking as he moved about. She'd been even *more* attuned to his presence when he'd come downstairs and she'd heard him cross the living room. She'd stayed in the kitchen. Somehow that had just seemed safer…easier…less fraught with vibrations she didn't want to come to terms with.

Hearing her name on Mitch's lips was unsettling now, and she told herself she was just being silly. Yet, seconds later when she stepped into the living room and found him taking up space in his long-sleeved hoodie and jeans, she almost backed into the kitchen again.

Making herself move forward, shifting her eyes away from his, she spotted the twenty-inch monitor on a side table. One moment she glimpsed one white crib with pink trim and green bedding. The next he'd pressed a button and she spotted the other crib with its pink-and-yellow designs. She could watch both babies by changing the channel.

"The wonders of technology." A smile shone in his voice.

She knew Mitch was good with electronics and especially computers. He was the first at the office to understand a new system, to fix glitches, to teach someone else the intricacies of a program.

"Are systems like this a side hobby for you?"

"Always have been. I'm self-taught. The skills come in handy now and then."

As long as she'd known Mitch, he'd downplayed what he did and who he helped. "You're a good man, Mitch."

He looked surprised for a moment.

She added, "If you can do something for someone else, you do."

"Lily, don't make so much of setting up a monitoring system."

Telling herself she should stay right where she was, she didn't listen to her better judgment. She advanced closer to Mitch and this time didn't look away. "You're not just helping *me*. It's sort of an attitude with you. If someone has a problem, you take time to listen."

Maybe he could see she was serious about this topic. Maybe he could see that she was trying to determine exactly how much help she should accept from him. Maybe he could see that this conversation was important to her. Nevertheless, by his silence he seemed reluctant to give away even a little piece of himself.

"Does it have something to do with being in Iraq?" she asked softly.

The flicker of response in his eyes told her she'd hit the mark. She saw one of his hands curve into a fist and she thought he might simply tell her it was none of her business. Instead, however, he lifted his shoulders in a shrug, as if this wasn't important. As if he didn't mind her asking at all.

"I survived," he told her calmly. "I figured there was a reason for that. I returned home with a new understanding of patience, tolerance and simple kindness."

Although Mitch's expression gave away nothing, Lily knew he was holding back. He was giving her an edited version of what he felt and what he'd experienced.

"Have you ever talked about Iraq?"

"No."

"Not even with your buddies?"

"They know what it was like. I don't have to talk about it."

She supposed that was true. Yet from the tension she could sense in Mitch, she understood he had scars that were more than skin deep.

With a tap on the control sitting next to the monitor on the table, he suggested, "Let me show you the remote and what the lights mean."

Discussion over. No matter what she thought, Mitch was finished with that topic, and he was letting her know it. She could push. But she sensed that Mitch wasn't the type of man who *could* be pushed. He would just shut down. That wouldn't get her anywhere at all. Why was she so hell-bent on convincing him that the bad stuff would only damage him if he kept it inside?

She'd let the conversation roll his way for now. For the next few minutes she let him explain the lights on the remote and how she could carry it into the kitchen with her and upstairs to her bedroom. When he handed it to her, their fingers skidded against each other and she practically jumped. She was so startled by the jolt of adrenaline it gave her, she dropped the remote.

She stooped over to retrieve it at the same time he crouched down. Their faces were so close together… close enough to kiss…

They moved apart and Lily let him grasp the control.

After Mitch picked it up, he handed it to her and quickly stepped away. "I'd better get going," he said. "Do you want me to turn off the system?"

"I can do it."

He nodded, crossing to the door, picking up the tool-box he'd set there.

She followed him, feeling as if something had gone

wrong, yet not knowing what. "Thank you again for the monitoring system. I really appreciate it."

"Are you going to be alone tomorrow?"

"No. Raina's coming to visit. She's going to drive me to the hospital so I can spend time with the twins while she makes rounds."

"That sounds like a plan. I'm glad you have friends you can count on."

"I am, too."

As their gazes found each other, his dark brown eyes deeply calm, Lily felt shaken up.

"If you need help when you bring the babies home, you have my number."

Yes, she did. But the way she was feeling right now, she wasn't going to use it. She couldn't call on him again when she felt attracted to him. That's what it was, plain and simple—attraction she was trying to deny. Oh, no. She wouldn't be calling his number anytime soon. She would not feel guilty believing she was being unfaithful to her husband's memory.

Maybe Mitch realized some of that, because he left.

Even though a cold wind blew into the foyer, Lily stood there watching Mitch's charcoal SUV back out of the driveway. When his taillights finally faded into the black night, she closed the door, relieved she was alone with her memories...relieved she might not see Mitch for a while.

Then everything would go back to normal between them.

Over the next few weeks Mitch didn't see much of Lily, though he stopped in at the hospital NICU almost every day. A few days ago, the twins had been moved to the regular nursery. This morning he'd run into Angie, who told him they'd gone home. Lily hadn't called him. Because she was overwhelmed with bringing the twins home and everything that entailed? Or because she wanted to prove to herself she could be a single mom and manage just fine?

He was going to find out.

When Mitch reached the Victorian, he scanned the house and grounds. Everything *seemed* normal—until he approached the front door. Although it was closed, he could hear the cries of two babies inside. New mothers had enough trouble handling one, let alone two. But where were Lily's friends?

With no response when he rang the doorbell, he knocked. When Lily still didn't answer, he turned the knob—no one in Sagebrush locked their doors—and stepped inside.

Immediately he realized the wails were coming from a room down the hall from the living room. Turning that way, he found the room that had been the women's exercise room. Now it looked like a makeshift nursery. There were two bassinets, a card table he assumed Lily used for changing the twins, and a scarred wooden rocking chair that looked as if it could be an antique. His gaze was quickly drawn to her. He knew he should look away from Lily's exposed breast as she tried to feed one baby while holding the other. Respectful of her as a new mom, he dropped his gaze to an odd-looking pillow on her lap, one of those nursing pillows advertised in baby magazines. But it didn't seem to be doing much good. Lily looked about ready to scream herself.

When she raised her head and saw him, she practically

had to yell over the squalls. "I couldn't come to the door. I can't seem to satisfy them," she admitted, her voice catching.

Without hesitating, Mitch took Sophie from her mom's arms, trying valiantly to ignore Lily's partially disrobed condition. He had enough trouble with the visions dancing through his head at night. Concentrating for the moment on Sophie, he flipped a disposable diaper from a stack, tossed it onto his shoulder and held the infant against him. The feel of that warm little girl on his shoulder blanked out any other pictures. Taking in a whiff of her baby lotion scent, he knew nothing in the world could be as innocent and sweet as a newborn baby. His hand rubbed up and down her little back, and miraculously she began to quiet. In a few moments, her sobs subsided into hiccups.

Lily, a bit amazed, quickly composed herself and tossed a blanket over her shoulder to hide her breast. Then she helped Grace suckle once more. This time the baby seemed content.

"Did your friends desert you?" He couldn't imagine them doing that.

"No, of course not. Gina and Raina were here most of the day. When Angie got ready for work and left, Sophie and Grace were asleep."

Mitch watched as Lily took a deep breath and let it out slowly. "But they woke up, crying to be fed at the same time."

"Do you have milk in the fridge?"

"Yes, but—"

"Breast-feeding two babies is something that's going to take practice. In the meantime, I can give Sophie a bottle." He gestured to her lap. "Nursing pillows and experts' advice might work for some people, but you've got to be practical. There is no right way and wrong way to do this, Lily. You just have to do what works for you and the babies."

"How do you know so much about babies?" Lily asked in a small voice, looking down at her nursing child rather than at him.

His part in the practice was science-oriented and mostly behind the scenes. "Training," he said simply, remembering his rotation in obstetrics years ago.

That drew her eyes to his. He added, "And...sometimes in the field, you have to learn quickly." In Iraq, he'd helped a new mother who'd been injured, returning her and her newborn to her family.

Before Lily could ask another question, he gently laid Sophie in one of the bassinets and hurried to the kitchen to find her milk. A short time later he carried one of the kitchen chairs to the nursery and positioned it across from Lily. Then he picked up Sophie again and cradled her in his arm. They sat in silence for a few minutes as both twins took nourishment.

"What made you stop by today?" Lily finally asked.

Lily's blond hair was fixed atop her head with a wooden clip. Wavy strands floated around her face. She was dressed in a blue sweater and jeans and there was a slight flush to her cheeks. Because he was invading private moments between her and her babies?

"I was at the hospital and found out they were discharged today."

Lily's eyes grew wider. Did she think he was merely checking up on her so he could say he had? He wished! He was in this because she'd gotten under his skin.

"Feeding these two every three hours, or more often, could get complicated. What would you have done if I hadn't arrived?"

"I would have figured something out."

Her stubbornness almost convinced him to shock her by taking her into his arms and kissing her. Lord, where had that thought come from? "I'm sure Gina and Raina never would have left if they knew you were so overwhelmed."

"Raina and Gina have families."

"They also both have nannies," he reminded her.

"They also both have—"

Mitch knew Lily had been about to say that they both had husbands. Instead, she bit her lower lip and transferred Grace to her other breast, taking care to keep herself covered with the blanket.

"I'm sorry I just walked in on you like that." He might as well get what happened out in the open or they'd both have that moment between them for a while.

"I'm going to have to get over my privacy issues if I intend to breast-feed them for very long. I sat down with the accountant last week. I can take a leave for seven or eight months and be okay financially. My practice is important, but I really feel as if I need to be with them to give them a good start in life."

Since she was the only parent they had, he could certainly understand that.

"Do you think the practice can do without me for that long?"

"We can manage. You know our client list is down because of insurance issues. This could work out to everyone's advantage. We can always consult with you from home if we need your expertise."

Suddenly remembering the need to burp Sophie, he set the bottle on the floor and balanced the tiny baby on his knee. His hand was practically as large as *she* was. What would life be like taking care of them every day? Being able to watch their progress and all the firsts? Keeping his palm on her chest, he rubbed her back until she burped.

Smiling at Lily he said offhandedly, "She's easy."

Lily smiled back.

In that moment, he knew being here with Lily like this was dangerous.

What he was about to suggest was even *more* dangerous.

Chapter Four

"Do you want me to sleep on the couch again to-night?" Mitch asked as he cradled Sophie in his arm once more and offered her the bottle again. He couldn't help studying her perfect baby features. He was beginning to recognize a warm feeling that enveloped his heart when he was around Sophie and Grace.

After a lengthy pause, he cast a sideways glance at Lily to gauge her expression. As long as she was upstairs and he stayed downstairs, he wouldn't worry her with the restlessness that plagued him at night.

She looked somber as she debated with herself about what to say. He could almost hear her inner conversation because he'd already had the same one. If he stayed, they'd connect more. If he stayed, they might get to know each other better.

Quietly, she responded, "If you stay, I think I can

keep Sophie and Grace happier. The two of us are obviously handling them better than *I* was handling them alone. I have to learn what works and what doesn't. That will just take time. In the meantime, I want to stay calm. I want to enjoy both of them. I can't go into a panic just because Grace and Sophie are crying at the same moment."

"Why *did* you panic?" Extreme reactions weren't at all like Lily. But she'd never been a mom before. She bit her lower lip and he found himself focused on her mouth much too intensely.

"I have these two little beings depending on me twenty-four hours a day, seven days a week," she attempted to explain. "I don't want to let them down. I don't want either of them to feel neglected."

It was easy to see Lily had already bonded with her daughters and she wanted nothing to interfere with those bonds, not even another willing pair of hands giving her aid. He attempted to be reasonable, realizing he wanted to stay more than he wanted to go. "Right now, they need to have their basic needs met—feeding, changing and cuddling. They'll learn to know you," he reassured her quickly. "They won't mind if someone else gives them what they need. In a few months, they'll both be more particular. They'll want you when they want you. So for now, take advantage of the fact that someone else can help."

"You make it sound so simple," she said with a wry smile. "And we know it isn't."

No, nothing was simple. Besides the sheer enormity of the twins' birth, other feelings besides affection for Sophie and Grace were developing between him and Lily. However, neither of them were going to mention

those. No. They wouldn't be having that discussion anytime soon...which left the door wide open for his desire
to cause trouble. Yet he still wanted to be close to her.

As he set Sophie on his knee to burp her again,
he asked, "Will you take the babies upstairs to sleep
tonight?"

"Yes. I want them to get used to their cribs. I've got
to get the hang of breast-feeding both of them, but that
might be easier to juggle during the day. I thought I might
put a small refrigerator upstairs for night feedings."

"That sounds like a good idea. Maybe I can go pick
one up for you tomorrow."

"But I'm paying for it."

"Okay, you're paying for it." He knew better than to
argue.

With her gaze locked on his, he felt a turning so deep
inside of him that he had to stand with Sophie and walk
her back and forth across the room. She'd drunk three
ounces of the bottle and that was good. Taking her to
the card table, he unsnapped her Onesies so he could
change her.

"Mitch, you don't have to do that."

He glanced over his shoulder while he held Sophie
with one hand and picked up a diaper with the other. "I
don't mind changing her. But if you'd rather I didn't, I
won't."

Mitch guessed Grace was still locked on Lily's breast.
Just imagining that—

"As long as *you* don't mind," Lily finally said.

He seemed to be all thumbs with the small diaper,
but he hoped Lily wasn't noticing. The tiny snaps on
the Onesies were a challenge, too, but his left hand had

almost become as proficient as his right hand had once been—before shrapnel had torn into it.

Finally Sophie was ready for bed. Her little eyes were practically closed and her angelic face was peaceful. "I'll carry her upstairs and lay her in her crib. You can come up when Grace finishes."

"I have receiving blankets up there on the side of each crib. Can you swaddle her in one? They're supposed to sleep better if I do that."

"I'll try it."

"And you have to lay her on her back."

"I know, Lily."

She flushed.

"After I put her to bed, I'll pull out a blanket and a pillow for the sofa. I remember where you got them."

Lily nodded, but dropped her eyes to Grace and didn't look at him. If they didn't admit to the intimacy developing between them, then the intimacy wouldn't exist, right?

Right.

They were tiptoeing along a line in the sand, hoping neither one of them fell onto the other side.

He let out a pent-up breath he didn't even know he was holding when he left the downstairs nursery and headed up the steps, Sophie sleeping against his shoulder. The hall light guided him into the babies' room, where he grabbed the blanket and carefully wrapped Sophie in it on the changing table, murmuring softly to her as he did. Then he gently laid her in her crib and switched on the monitoring system.

After turning on the castle night-light by the rocker, he went to the hall for his bedding. At the closet, he glanced back at the room, almost ready to return and wish the little girl a good night. But he knew he couldn't become attached, not to the babies any more than to Lily. Nothing was permanent. Everything ended. He had no right to even think about Lily in a romantic way. He had no intention of making life more complicated for either of them.

After Mitch went downstairs, he made up the sofa and sat on it, staring at the monitor. Sophie did look like a cherub with her wispy blond hair, her blue eyes, her little body that seemed more heavenly than earthly. Her tiny face turned from left to right and he wondered if she missed Grace already.

He was so engrossed in his reflections that he didn't hear Lily come into the living room until the floor squeaked. She was holding Grace in a sling that kept her nestled against her chest.

"Is Sophie asleep?" Lily asked.

"Come see."

"I have to put Grace down, too."

"A couple of minutes won't matter. Come here."

Lily just stared at Sophie, her sweet sleep as entrancing as her little nose, long eyelashes and broad brow. "The monitor is wonderful, Mitch," Lily said in a low voice. "But they're so small. I'll probably be going in every fifteen minutes to check on them."

"You need your sleep. I'll be watching from down here. How about if I stay awake until the first feeding?"

"You need your sleep, too."

"I'm used to not sleeping. I was a trauma surgeon, remember?"

She remembered and unintentionally her gaze went to his arm and his hand.

Self-consciously, he moved it and balled it into a fist. Though he expected her to move away, she didn't.

"Do you think about what you used to do very often?"

"Often enough. But that was then and this is now. Why don't I walk you upstairs? We'll make sure both babies are settled."

Lily took one last look at the image on the monitor and then crossed to the stairway. Mitch waited a beat or so and then followed her.

Upstairs, by the glow of the night-light, Lily took Grace from her carrier and wrapped her in a blanket as Mitch had done with Sophie. After Lily laid Grace in her crib, she stooped over the baby and kissed her forehead. "I love you, sweet girl. I'm glad you're home."

Then she moved to Sophie's crib and did the same.

Aware Mitch hadn't come far into the room, Lily glanced at him as he stood by the chair, his arms crossed over his chest—watchful and distant.

When he'd arrived at the house earlier and come into the downstairs nursery, she'd felt so many emotions that they'd tumbled over each other. Yes, she'd been embarrassed. But she'd also felt a little proud. Only a few moments had passed until she'd realized she *should* feel embarrassed. And then she had.

As they'd put the babies to bed, though, the situation had seemed right. Mitch handled them so well... so comfortably...so like a father. Sometimes she could see the affection he felt for them. But other times, he removed himself.

Like now.

He fell into step beside her as she left the nursery

and walked down the hall to her bedroom. At her door, she was ready to say good-night, ready to fall into bed, exhausted from the stress, the worry and the joy of bringing the babies home today. Yet a simple good-night didn't seem adequate and when she gazed into Mitch's eyes, she couldn't look away.

He seemed to have the same problem.

There was something about him standing there, perfectly still, his shoulders wide enough to block the doorway, his height filling the space. Maybe it was the sight of him without his tie and with the first few buttons of his white shirt open. Maybe it was her reaction to the black chest hair peeking out. Maybe she thought about all he'd done for her. Maybe, for just a short time, she gave in to the thought that she might *need* someone to watch out for her. She only knew that thoughts weren't running through her brain as fast as heat was flashing through her body. She wasn't thinking at all when she leaned forward. Rather, she was feeling and wishing and hoping and remembering what it had felt like to be held by a man.

Her babies were so little. Her life had been torn apart. In the midst of caring for her girls and forging ahead, her attraction to Mitch seemed to be a living, breathing entity that at that moment she couldn't deny.

When his strong arms enfolded her, she felt safe. As he murmured her name, she felt cared for. He lowered his head and she lifted her chin. Their lips met.

Lily's senses whirled and she couldn't deny a longing that came from deep within. As Mitch's mouth opened over hers, she lost all sense of time and place. All she cared about was now, the rush of wanting, the scent of

Mitch that was new and exciting, the thrill of feeling like a woman again.

Suddenly her womb tightened as it did when she nursed the babies. Troy's daughters.

What in God's name was she doing?

As suddenly as the kiss began, she tore away. The expression on Mitch's face told her he knew why. She clamped her hand over her lips and tears rushed to her eyes. She saw that determined look come over Mitch and she couldn't face it, not tonight.

"Talk to me, Lily," he coaxed gently.

She shook her head. "I can't. Not now. Maybe in the morning."

"Do you want to let us both stew all night when what you need is sleep?"

"It was a mistake."

He sighed. "Maybe that's one of the things we need to talk about."

When she remained silent, he stroked a tear from her cheek, finally agreeing. "All right. Go to bed. I'll be here if you need help with the babies during the night."

"Mitch, I'm sorry."

He put his finger gently over her lips.

Backing into her room, she closed the door. She heard his boots on the wooden floorboards, his tread as he walked down the stairs. Then she collapsed on her bed, not even taking her clothes off, shutting her eyes and praying sleep would come quickly.

The following morning, Mitch made scrambled eggs while Angie and Lily fed the twins in the upstairs nursery.

He'd crossed the line last night. He'd known physical

contact with Lily was taboo. But it hadn't been until his lips had touched hers that he'd realized how truly vulnerable she was.

He'd damaged their relationship and he didn't know if he could fix it. But he had to get the old one back—he'd made a promise to Troy.

When Angie had arrived home after midnight, the twins had been starting to stir. She said she'd help him feed them so Lily could sleep. But Lily had heard them, come in, taken Grace from Angie and told her to go to bed. She'd hardly glanced at him.

They'd fed Grace and Sophie in silence. When the twins woke again at four, they'd both fed them again. Mitch had never actually appreciated how complicated this was for women. They hadn't recovered completely from giving birth and they had to use reserves they didn't know they had to combat sleep deprivation, fatigue and chores that seemed to multiply with each hour.

And what had he done? Stirred up something that was better left alone. He didn't know if Lily was ever going to look him in the eyes again.

He'd just switched off the burner when she and Angie rolled in a double stroller. Grace and Sophie looked as if they were content and almost asleep.

Crossing to the refrigerator, Angie pulled out milk and orange juice, snagging the coffeepot and bringing it to the table. "You should go back to bed," Angie told Lily as they pulled out their chairs.

"I have laundry to do, and I want to make up a couple of casseroles and freeze them so we can just pull them out this week if we need them."

Although Mitch sat at the table with them, Lily

glanced down at her plate. She picked up a slice of toast, took a bite and set it down again.

For the next ten minutes, the lump in Mitch's chest grew as he and Angie made conversation.

Finally, his breakfast eaten, he asked Lily, "Can I talk to you for a minute before I go?"

Her attention automatically went to her daughters, but Angie reassured her quickly. "I'll watch them. Go ahead."

There were so many things he wanted to tell Lily as they stood in the foyer. But he couldn't think of one. She was wearing jeans and a pink sweater and looked as if she were going to face the new day with determination and courage, the way she always did.

He knew what she wanted to hear from him, so he said it. "You were right. Last night was a mistake. I was out of line."

"You weren't the one who started it," she admitted honestly. "I don't know what got into me."

"You were grateful for a little help," he said with a smile that didn't come from inside.

"A *lot* of help," she returned, gazing into his eyes like she used to.

"Are you going to be okay when Angie leaves for work?"

"I'll be fine. It's Raina's day off. She's coming over."

He nodded, sure her friends would give her any help she needed, at least for a while. But he also knew Lily wouldn't want to burden them and she'd soon be taking all of it on herself.

They couldn't get involved for so many reasons. What if Lily ever saw his scars, learned his fears? The last relationship he'd tried a few years ago hadn't worked because of all of it. Nothing had changed since then, and on Lily's part, her grief and her connection to Troy was sustaining her in some ways. Missing and longing for him meant loving him. She wasn't ready to let go of that. Still, Mitch didn't know how to walk away from her. He couldn't because he'd promised he wouldn't.

"I'll call you in a couple of days, just to see if Grace and Sophie are settling in. If you need anything, you have my number."

She reached out and touched his arm, probably feeling the same wall he did, a wall they were both standing behind so they wouldn't get hurt.

"Thank you," she said softly.

He left the Victorian again, realizing he didn't want her thanks. What he *did* want was still a mystery to him.

A few weeks later, Mitch was driving home from work when he decided to call Lily. They'd had a *brief* phone conversation last week because neither was comfortable with what had happened and they couldn't seem to get back on that "friend" footing. Now her cell phone rang and rang and rang until finally—a man picked up.

"Who is this?" Mitch asked, surprised by the male voice. A repairman, maybe? But why would he have Lily's cell phone?

"This is Craig Gillette. I'm the manager of Sagebrush Foods."

"Sagebrush Foods? I don't understand. Where's Lily Wescott?"

"Mrs. Wescott had an incident in our store. She's okay now but…"

An incident? What the hell was that? "Put her on," Mitch ordered.

Apparently speaking to the authority in Mitch's voice, the man said, "Sir, I can't right now. We've got two crying infants and she's feeling a little dizzy."

Dizzy? "You tell her not to move. I'll be there in five." Mitch didn't give the manager time to protest or approve. He stepped on the gas.

Minutes later Mitch rushed into the store, scanning the produce area. Rounding a corner, he spotted Lily in the canned goods aisle, holding a paper cup. There were cans of green beans all over the floor around the folding chair where she sat. The twins were ensconced in their stroller. Sophie's little face was screwed up in displeasure, but Grace seemed content for the moment to stare at the bright lights and rows of colorful cans.

Mitch let his training prevail rather than the fear that threatened his composure. In as calm a voice as he could muster, he asked, "What happened?" followed by, "Are you all right?"

Lily looked so pale, and all he wanted to do was lift her into his arms and carry her somewhere safe. But the twins were a concern, too, and he had to get to the bottom of what had happened.

"I just felt a little dizzy, that's all," she said in a soft voice, taking another sip of water. "I haven't gotten much sleep lately and I ran out of diapers…" Grace reached out a little hand to her and Lily reached back.

He got the picture much too well and he didn't like what he saw. His guess? She'd felt faint and she'd run the stroller into the corner of the green beans display.

"Did she pass out?" he asked Gillette.

"No, sir. We wanted to call an ambulance, but she said she just needed to put her head down between her knees for a while—" He stopped when Lily gave him a scolding look as if he were divulging too much information.

Mitch went to Lily and crouched down beside her, looking her over with a practiced doctor's eye. "Be honest with me. Do I need to call an ambulance?"

There were deep blue smudges under both of her eyes. Her hair was a disheveled ponytail and she wore a sweatsuit. This wasn't the Lily he was used to, with her composed attitude, neat hairdos and tailored clothing.

Looking up at him, she forced a smile. She was clearly exhausted.

With his fingertips to her neck, he felt her pulse beating fast.

"Mitch," she protested, turning her head.

His fingers stayed put. "Quiet for a few seconds," he suggested.

Her pulse was definitely racing.

"No ambulance," she said.

"Then tell me what's going on. But drink that water before you do." He guessed she was dehydrated.

"You're acting like a doctor."

"I'm also acting like a friend."

Their gazes met and Mitch could see she was remembering their kiss as vividly as he was, even in these circumstances. Just friends? Not likely.

She didn't argue with him, but rather drank the cup of water.

"Are you still dizzy? Should I call Hillary?" Their colleague was her OB/GYN.

"No. I'm seeing her in a few days for a follow-up.
I know what's wrong, Mitch. Not enough sleep, not
enough liquids, probably not enough food. I forget to
eat when I'm busy. Please don't scold."

He would have, but he could see she realized
what he'd known could happen all along—she was
overwhelmed.

"Let's see if you can stand on your own."

He held her around the waist and helped her to her
feet. She felt slight to him. She'd definitely lost weight.
He should have been checking in with her daily, no
matter how uncomfortable things were between them.
So much for looking after her.

His body was responding in ways it shouldn't as he
kept his arm around her waist and they walked a few
steps down the aisle.

"Do you think you can walk to your car on your own
steam? I'll drive yours then walk back here for mine."

"I drove over here for the diapers because I didn't
want to bother anyone," she muttered, then added
fiercely, "I'm capable of walking to the car."

At least she wasn't protesting him driving her home.
He wanted her to understand the seriousness of what
was happening to her. But that discussion would have
to wait until she was on the sofa with her feet up and
Sophie and Grace were fed and diapered.

In the house a while later, they sat on the sofa, hips
practically touching, watching the babies in their cribs
on the monitor. Mitch had found laundry in the washer
and dryer, bottles in the sink, and had coaxed a little
information from Lily. The babies now had a fussy spell
that lasted from after Angie left in the evening until well
after midnight. And they were nursing at least every

three hours. She *was* exhausted and dehydrated and had to do more to take care of herself. But she couldn't do that unless the twins needs were met first.

Mitch began, "You need help, Lily, and you've got to get it before you can't take care of Sophie and Grace. Hire an au pair who will stay at the house for free rent."

He shifted so they weren't quite so close as he expected Lily to protest. She didn't. Rather, she just looked pensive. "I really hadn't thought about doing that. I don't know if Angie would like having a stranger move in."

"She can probably see you need help, too, but doesn't know what to do about it. Talk to her. Talk to Raina and Gina. Maybe they'll know of someone who needs a job and is good with children. But you can't go on like this."

"I know. Believe me, Mitch, I do. What just happened scared me. I just wish—" She swallowed hard. "If Troy were here—"

Mitch watched as she blinked fast and faced the cold splash of reality once more. He didn't know whether to cover her hand with his or move even farther away. Everything had become so complicated between them.

After a few moments of silence, Lily seemed to pull herself together. "Thinking about Troy…" She stopped. "His sister Ellie might be the perfect person to help me."

"Isn't she in Oklahoma?"

"Yes, but Troy's mom and Ellie have wanted to visit. Maybe they could come and help out and maybe…" A smile bloomed on Lily's lips. "Maybe Ellie could stay! She could set up her web business from here. I'm going to call Angie first. If she's agreeable, then I'll phone Ellie."

Lily picked up the handset from the end table.

As she dialed a number, Mitch realized he should be happy she was going to get the help she needed. Yet part of him knew that if Troy's sister came to assist her, Lily could stay entrenched in the past instead of moving on.

That shouldn't matter to him. But it did.

Chapter Five

Lily hung up the receiver and glanced at the glass of juice Mitch had brought her, now empty. She knew better than to let herself become dehydrated. She knew better about a lot of things. She should be grateful Mitch had called right when he had. Troy had always maintained, *There are no coincidences.* She'd always laughed when he'd said it, but maybe he was right.

She found Mitch in the laundry room, pulling baby clothes from the dryer. "You don't have to do that," she said.

He just arched one heavy brow at her and removed the last of the Onesies, settling them in the wash basket.

"I ordered takeout from the Yellow Rose." He glanced at his watch. "It should be here in about fifteen minutes."

"Takeout? But they don't deliver unless—"

"I ordered two dinners for tonight, and three more. You should have enough for a few days so you don't have to worry about cooking."

She knew better than to protest. She should have ordered food herself. She'd intended to cook, but with Angie on the late shift, it had seemed a bother when she had so many other things to do. Still, almost fainting had scared her. She had to eat, drink and get some rest.

"That was a long phone conversation," Mitch commented, carrying the laundry basket into the kitchen and then the living room.

"Just set it on the coffee table," she said. "I have to divide the clothes. I keep some down here, and the rest upstairs."

After he set it down, he asked, "So is the cavalry coming?"

She smiled. "Troy's mother is going to stay for a week. She doesn't want to leave his dad for longer than that. But Ellie will drive her here and stay as long as I need her. She said she could use a change of scene, and Texas seems like a good spot. She's going to bring her sewing machine and make baby clothes and get her website up and running while she's here. If the three of us get along well, she might stay indefinitely."

"I assume since she makes baby clothes, she likes babies."

"She worked at a day-care center for a while, so she's had more practical experience than *I* have."

"I'm glad that's settled. When are they coming?"

"Next week."

"And in the meantime?"

"In the meantime, I'll get by. But I'll take better care of myself."

"That's a promise?"

"It's a promise."

There was about six inches of space between them that seemed to be filled with all kinds of electricity. Lily couldn't understand why, when she was around Mitch now, every nerve in her body tingled a new message.

"Why don't you take out the clothes you want to keep down here, and I'll carry the rest upstairs."

She took a few outfits from the basket and laid them on the coffee table. As Mitch lifted it again, she found her hand going to his forearm.

He pulled away and she realized she'd clasped his scarred and injured arm. "I'm sorry," she said.

He put down the laundry and took a step closer to her. "There's nothing to be sorry about. I'm just not used to having anyone touch me there."

"Does it hurt?"

"No."

"Do you ever let anyone see it?" She didn't know why the personal question had rolled off her tongue so easily, but what had happened at the grocery store had solidified the bond between them.

"Do you?" she prodded. "You wear long sleeves, winter and summer."

"Why does it matter?"

"Because we're friends and I'd like to know."

His expression remained steady, his voice steely. "Most people can't handle seeing scars. They're fascinated by them, but they're afraid of them. They want to ask questions, but they turn away."

"Do you think I'd turn away?"

The two of them were breathing the same air, standing in the same space, but a shield went up in Mitch's eyes that sent him somewhere apart from her. Suddenly she suspected why.

"Have you been in a relationship since you returned from Iraq?"

He started to swivel away from her to go into the kitchen. She wouldn't let him evade her that easily. She didn't touch him this time, but just slipped in front of him so he couldn't take another step without running into her.

"Lily," he said with exasperation. "I don't want to talk about it."

"Have you ever talked about it...talked about *her?*"

"No."

"Just as you haven't talked about Iraq."

"That's right."

Men! Lily thought. Troy had been the same way. He hadn't spoken to her about his earlier deployments, and she hadn't pushed. She had imagined that he'd eventually confide in her. But they hadn't had time. And maybe if he had confided in her, she would have been more prepared—

"So don't talk about Iraq," she conceded.

"But tell you about my love life?" Mitch asked, almost amused.

She realized how ridiculous she was being, when Mitch was a private man who didn't reveal much at all! "I guess I just need something to think about besides my own life right now."

That shield was still in his eyes but his face took on a gentler look.

"Okay. I'll do this once." He jammed his hands into his trouser pockets. "I was back over a year. I'd gotten a fellowship in endocrinology in Dallas and met Charlene, who was a reporter for the local news. She wanted to do a story about my new specialty and why I was changing, but I told her no. After a few tries and a few conversations, we started going out. I wore long sleeves most of the time then, too. One night I took her out to dinner. Afterward, things progressed naturally but when we got to the bedroom and I took off my shirt— She couldn't bear to see my scars, let alone touch them. That's when I realized reality was just a little too difficult for most people to handle."

"Most *women*," Lily murmured, realizing how little emotion Mitch had put into that recital. "That's what you meant to say."

"Maybe I did."

"Not every woman is the same." She could see right away that he didn't believe that. "The scars are more extensive than on your arm and hand," she guessed.

"Yes. They're on my shoulder, back and side, too."

Lily thought about what he'd said but kept her gaze from falling to his shoulder, or to his flat stomach. She was feeling almost dizzy again. Could that be from imagining Mitch without his shirt? Was she different from that reporter? Would extensive scars make her want to turn away?

The doorbell rang.

Mitch took a step back, looking...relieved? Was *she* relieved that the personal conversation was over? Or did she *want* to delve deeper? Somehow she knew Mitch wouldn't let her do that. At least, not tonight.

"So what's for dinner?" she asked brightly, knowing the Yellow Rose delivery had arrived at the door.

Getting to know Mitch any better would mean ties

she might not want...problems she didn't need. Getting to know Mitch better could lead to another kiss.

Neither of them wanted that—right?

Lily's cavalry arrived and Mitch stayed away. He knew it was best for both of them.

Almost a month after the grocery store incident, he received a call as he sat at the desk in his spare bedroom, ready to check email and eat dinner—a slice of pizza and a beer. When he recognized the number on his cell phone, he quickly swallowed his mouthful of pizza and shut down his email program.

"Hey, Lily. How's it going?"

When he'd called to check on her a couple of weeks before, Troy's mother had just left Lily's home and Ellie was settling in. Mitch had known Lily didn't need him there, or even want him there. He knew what had probably gone on while Troy's family was with her—lots of remembering.

It was best that he stay on his side of town and not interfere.

"Darlene and Ellie have been wonderful. They gave me a chance to pull myself back together, get my diet straightened out and find a sleep schedule. And Ellie's definitely going to stay. Angie really likes her, and we all get along great."

After a long pause, she asked, "Why haven't you been over lately?"

"I really didn't think you needed another visitor. Besides, the practice is picking up. I've been working late many nights."

"The beginning of May is a time for growth and

thinking about the future. I can see why the practice picks up this time of year. I miss it."

"I thought you might."

"Don't get me wrong, I love taking care of Grace and Sophie. Doing that, even with Ellie here, is enough to keep me busy all day. But working with you and Hillary and Jon and the staff is part of my life, too."

"So you're coming back?"

"I have to, Mitch. I'm going to see how the summer goes with Ellie, then I'll give you all a definite date."

Lily sounded less frazzled, more peaceful, maybe even a bit happy. He guessed the babies were bringing her joy, not just work, and that was lifting her up, fulfilling her in a new way.

She went on, "They're both cooing. And they're fascinated by their mobiles. You've got to come see them, Mitch, and meet Ellie."

Ellie was Lily's family now, along with her friends. He would bet a week's pay that their first meeting was going to be...uncomfortable. He thought about what type of visit this should be, how much time he should spend with Ellie and Lily, how much time with the twins.

"Have you been out of the house much?"

"Nope. The twins keep me a prisoner," she said with a laugh. "Seriously. I went to the grocery store again last week. This time I made it without knocking anything over. But that's been about it."

"Would tomorrow night be convenient?" he asked. "I could meet Ellie, see how the babies have grown, then take you for a drive. In fact, we could drive to the lake to hear the outdoor concert. How does that sound?"

"That sounds wonderful! But you realize, don't you,

I'm going to have to call back here every fifteen minutes to see what the twins are doing."

"That's a mother's prerogative. Why don't you check with your housemates to see if they mind your leaving, then give me a call back. I think the concert will be a nice break for both of us."

"Your idea sounds perfect. I'll get back to you shortly."

"I'll talk to you soon," Mitch said and hung up.

He didn't know whether to hope for this idea to go through or not. It could become more than a casual outing. Then he grabbed hold of reality again. Not if they *wanted* only casual. After all, it would be easy to stay casual. Lily could tell him all about the memories she and Troy's mother and sister had stirred up during their visit.

Casual would be the theme of the evening.

"How long have you been working with Lily?" Ellie asked on Saturday evening.

He'd arrived a short time before and looked in on the twins, who'd been finishing their supper. They were asleep in their bassinets now and Lily had gone upstairs to change.

Studying Ellie, he noticed she wore her light brown hair in a short, glossy bob that swung against her cheek. The style accentuated her heart-shaped face. At twenty-six, she was ten years younger than the brother she obviously missed.

Mitch tried to answer her question without becoming defensive. After all, who could blame her for watching out for her sister-in-law. "We've worked together for two and a half years."

"Troy mentioned you," she admitted. "Something about playing pool at the Silver Spur Grill."

"We did."

"He said you were in Iraq and had to leave the Guard for medical reasons." She looked him over as if expecting to find his injury and her gaze settled on his hand. She quickly looked away.

"I did," he answered crisply, not intending to go into *that*, even for Troy's sister. The screws the doctor had put in his shoulder and leg, his missing spleen, never mind the damage to his arm and hand, had shut down his ability to serve. Most of the time, no one could tell he'd been injured.

It was time to go on the offensive with Ellie. "Lily tells me you worked in a day-care setting."

"For a while," she responded.

If he got her talking, she might relax. "But you like to sew?"

Looking surprised that he knew a detail like that, she responded, "I started making customized outfits for gifts for friends and relatives. They became so popular, I was getting orders. That's when I decided to open the store. At first I did pretty well, but then when harder times hit, even folks who had the money for those kind of clothes decided to spend it elsewhere."

"I hope your web-based business takes off for you."

"I hope so, too. But in the meantime, I'm going to enjoy taking care of Grace and Sophie. Did you spend much time with them when you brought Lily home from the hospital?"

She clearly wasn't giving up on turning over every leaf of his association with Lily. But he didn't have anything to hide—not really. "Two babies are a handful. That's why I think it's important Lily get away for a bit tonight."

Ellie's green eyes canvassed his face as if searching for motives. Finally, she admitted, "I'm glad the weather turned warm enough."

At that moment, Lily came down the stairs.

Automatically, Mitch turned her way. She was wearing blue jeans and a red blouse with a yellow windbreaker tossed over her arm. She'd fashioned her hair with a clip at the nape and she looked...fantastic. Her blue eyes seemed even bluer tonight as she gave him a tentative smile. He couldn't look away and she seemed to be as immobilized as he was...

...Until Ellie cleared her throat and asked, "How long do you think the concert will last?"

Lily burst into motion, as if in denial that the moment of awareness had ever happened. "Oh, we won't stay for the whole concert, and I'll call in to check with you. That's the nice thing about going to the lake. I don't have to worry about anybody being bothered if I make phone calls during the concert. Since this is the first concert of the season, the audience will be sparse. So call me if the least little thing is wrong, or you think I should come home."

Lily talked very fast when she was nervous, and that's what she was doing now. Her last comment led him to wonder if she was looking for an excuse not to go. Was it because she was still uncomfortable since their kiss? He'd find out shortly.

Lily gave Ellie a list of instructions along with phone numbers, then hiked the strap of her purse over her shoulder, took a last look at the monitor, blew a kiss to the image of her daughters and went out the door.

On the drive to the lake they didn't talk, but rather enjoyed the peaceful scenery—ranches and cotton fields that spread as far as the eye could see, tumbleweeds rolling by.

After he turned off the main road, down a gravel lane, and bumped over a dusty area used as the parking space for the concert, Lily finally said, "I think I'd forgotten how green everything is at this time of year, how spring smells, how the sky turns purple and orange at sunset. In some ways, I feel like I've been locked in a closet since last summer, not really seeing what was around me. Except the twins, of course."

"You've faced a lot of change in the past ten months."

She lowered her window and took a huge breath of outside air as the May breeze tossed her hair. "I don't want to go back into that closet again."

"Then don't. You have help now. While you're on leave, take some time for yourself, too. Figure out who you are again in your new life."

Turning to him, she reached for his arm, and he guessed she didn't even realize she'd done that. "You've been through this, haven't you?" she asked.

Her fingers on his forearm seemed to send fire through his body. Trying to smother it, he responded roughly, "You know I have. I'm not sure major life change is anything anyone welcomes, especially when it's borne from tragedy."

He gently tugged away from her touch. "Come on. Let's go to this concert."

His body still racing with adrenaline from their

contact, Mitch pulled a blanket from the backseat. They headed toward the people gathering in a large pavilion. They didn't see anyone they knew as Mitch dropped the blanket on one of the park benches facing the bandstand. The sides of the pavilion would block the wind and Lily could always wrap herself in the blanket if she got cold.

Their shoulders brushed. Mitch considered moving away, but didn't. Still, he was glad they hadn't recognized anyone. He didn't want Lily having second thoughts about coming. Something told him Ellie would be grilling her when she got back, and she'd have plenty of second thoughts then. He was just glad she'd accepted his invitation tonight, even if it was only to escape her figurative closet for a little while.

The quartet that performed with oboe, bass, clarinet and guitar played instrumental versions of popular songs. The crowd didn't grow much larger as Mitch was sure it would have if this had been a country-and-western or bluegrass band, or even an oldies night. But it suited his purpose to be here tonight with Lily, to listen to calm and easy music so she could relax. Even when she called home, no worry lines fanned her brow as Ellie reassured her that her girls were fine.

When Lily recognized a song, she hummed along. Her face was in profile as she gazed toward the lake, and he could study her without being afraid she'd catch him. Her hair waved in gentle curls under the barrette. Her turned-up nose was so recognizable on Sophie and Grace. Lily's bangs were long, brushed to one side, her brows a shade darker than her hair as they drew together when she concentrated on the music. She'd never worn much makeup, but tonight he noticed a sheen of gloss on her lips.

He could watch her all night and not tire of her expressions, the tilt of her head, the slant of her cheeks. He felt desire grip him again.

At that moment, she turned away from the music toward him...as if she wanted to sneak a peek at *his* expression. They both froze, their gazes locked, their bodies leaning just a little closer until the press of their shoulders was noticeable. Mitch reminded himself that there were so many reasons to keep away from Lily.

The music ended and the quartet announced a break.

Not moving away, Lily asked, "What do you think?"

About her? About the night? About the music? Which was the question to answer?

"My mother would have called them a dance band."

Lily blinked as if she hadn't expected that at all. But then she rallied. "Did she like to dance?"

Letting out a silent sigh of relief, Mitch leaned back so the pressure between their shoulders eased. "She didn't go out dancing, if that's what you mean. She didn't date. She always told me she didn't have time. She'd say, 'Who could work and have time for a man, too?'"

"A modern philosophy if I ever heard one," Lily joked.

Mitch chuckled. "Maybe so. But once in a while, she'd put on the radio and I'd catch her dancing around the kitchen. She always got embarrassed, but I could tell that if she'd had the time and a partner, she'd be good at it."

To his surprise, Mitch felt his phone vibrate against his hip. When he checked the caller ID, he recognized the number of a friend, Tony Russo. "I should take this," he said.

"Go ahead. We can go back to your SUV. I really should be getting home."

Because of that pulsating moment when he'd almost kissed her again? "You're sure?"

"Yes."

The certainty in her answer told him she didn't want to take the chance of staying longer, the chance that darkness and a starry sky might urge them to become more intimate.

A few minutes later, Lily stood beside Mitch at his SUV, wondering why she had agreed to come with him tonight. This seemed so much like a date and it just couldn't be! She'd known right away Ellie didn't approve when she'd told her where she was going.

She had to ask herself...would Troy approve of her being here with Mitch tonight? Troy's approval still mattered to her. She fingered her wedding ring, still feeling married.

Inhaling the scents of spring on the wind, she attempted to stay in the moment. She exhaled confusion and loss, in favor of life and music and the sliver of moon above. She was aware of Mitch's conversation, his deep laugh. He asked about someone named Jimmy and reported he'd gotten an email from Matt last week.

She was learning Mitch had more facets than she'd ever imagined. He had depth she'd never known about. He had a past he didn't want to talk about.

Now, however, when he ended his call, he smiled at

her. That smile both comforted her and made her breath hitch!

"An old friend?" she guessed, taking the safe route.

"Yes, Tony served with me in Iraq."

Surprised he was forthcoming about that, she asked, "Is he coming for a visit?"

"You heard me mention the bed-and-breakfast."

She nodded.

"Every year, the first weekend in December, I get together with servicemen I knew in Iraq. We alternate locations and their families come, too. This year it's my turn to host."

"What a wonderful idea!"

"We usually start planning this time of year to get the best airfares and accommodations. We have a money pool so if someone can't afford to come, the cash is there to draw on."

"How long does your reunion last?"

"Friday to Sunday. My house will be home base on Saturday. Do you have any ideas to occupy kids?"

"Besides enlisting someone to play Santa Claus?" she joked. "I used to do some face painting."

"You're kidding."

"No. I'm *not* just a doctor. I have an artistic bent."

He laughed. "That would be perfect."

A bit of moonlight drifted over them as they stood close. The look in Mitch's eyes was recognizable to her. He'd had that same look before he'd kissed her outside her bedroom.

When he reached out and stroked her cheek, she didn't pull away. She couldn't. There was something about Mitch that drew her to him, that made her want to forget her inhibitions, her idea of propriety, her sadness and loss.

"Lily," he murmured as the stars bore witness, as the moon seemed to tilt, as the ground trembled under her feet. The touch of his fingers on her face was filled with an aching longing.

But then he dropped his hand to his side and opened the passenger door. He didn't have to say anything and neither did she. They knew they couldn't kiss again. If they did, they might not stop there.

Ellie, Sophie and Grace were waiting for her. She didn't want to be any more confused when she walked in that door than she already was now.

Chapter Six

Time rolled by so fast, Lily could hardly count the days. She spent a lot of time thinking about Mitch, of how he'd touched her face at the lake. That night they'd silently but tacitly backed away from each other. Because of Ellie? Because they both feared their feelings were inappropriate?

The last week in May, Lily pushed Sophie and Grace's stroller into the office suite that was still familiar to her. Yet when she looked around at the sea-foam-green furniture, the rose carpeting and the green-and-mauve wallpaper, she didn't feel as if she *did* belong any more. She'd only been away three months, yet it seemed like a lifetime.

"This is where I work," she told Ellie, motioning to the reception area, the glass window behind which their receptionist Maryanne sat, the hall leading to exam rooms, office suites and the lab.

"It's really kind of…cozy," Ellie remarked as if she was surprised. "I think I expected white walls and tile and a sterile atmosphere."

"We try to keep it relaxed," Lily explained. "The couples and women who come to us are stressed enough. The more relaxed we can keep the process, the better."

"How many doctors work here?"

"Four, as well as two nurse-practitioners, two techs and our receptionist."

Lily rolled the stroller up to the receptionist's window.

Maryanne slid the glass open and grinned at her. "We miss you, Dr. Wescott," she said to Lily.

"I miss all of you, too," Lily returned, meaning it. Helping other women have babies was important to her, and even more so now, since she knew the joy of her twins.

She introduced Ellie.

Maryanne came out of her cubicle to coo over the babies. "They're adorable. I'm so glad you brought them in. And at just the right time. Everybody's on their lunch break. Go on back to the lounge."

Ellie took a peek down the hall. "Maybe I shouldn't go with you. I don't want to interrupt anything."

"Don't be silly," Lily said. "The practice is usually closed from twelve to one every day. That's why I was glad when we finished with Tessa right on time. I know Hillary will want to meet you. When I had a checkup with her, I told her about your baby store and your customized outfits. She has a one-year-old. She could be your first paying customer in Sagebrush."

Although Lily had attempted to prepare herself to see Mitch again, she didn't feel ready. Not after their awkward parting the evening of the concert.

As soon as she pushed open the door to the lounge and saw Mitch sitting at the table with Hillary and Jon, she was tossed back to that night, standing close to him by his SUV, the heat of his fingers a scalding impression on her cheek.

Mitch stood as soon as he spotted her and Ellie, the white lab coat he wore giving him the professional appearance that had been so familiar to her before the night of the banquet, before Grace and Sophie had been born.

The twins were the center of attention now as everyone crowded around. Lily was glad for that, relieved to be able to introduce Ellie to her colleagues, grateful that no one could see how being in the same room with Mitch affected her. Lily couldn't believe it herself. Maybe she just didn't want to believe it.

What kind of woman was she? She'd loved her husband, loved him to the moon and back. He'd only been gone for ten months. Many nights she still cried herself to sleep, missing him, needing him, longing for him. Her reaction to Mitch didn't make sense. Not at all. Before the twins were born, she'd never looked at him as anything but a colleague. But now, as everyone babbled to the babies and chatted politely with Ellie, Mitch's gaze passed over Lily's lilac top and slacks then swiftly returned to her face. His appraisal left her a little short of breath.

Hurriedly, she ducked her head and bent to scoop

Sophie from the stroller. "I don't know what I'd do without Ellie," she told everyone. "I seem to need six hands when these two are crying at the same time."

"So when are you coming back?" Hillary asked, her short chestnut hair fringing her face.

"Probably in November," she answered, not knowing what the next months would bring.

"You take your time deciding," Jon said. He was tall and lean with narrow black glasses that made him look scholarly.

Hillary asked, "May I hold Sophie?"

"Sure."

Hillary took the baby and settled her in the crook of her arm, looking down on her with the affection moms feel for kids. "I believe these little girls are going to be petite."

"Maybe. Or they could eventually grow as tall as Troy." Lily felt the need to mention his name, to bring him into the conversation.

Jon leaned a little closer to her. "How are you doing, really?"

"I'm okay. It's just the world's very different without Troy in it. Some days I expect that. Other days I expect him to come walking through the door, pick up Grace and Sophie, to figure out which one will look for his approval and which one won't."

Hillary had obviously overheard. She said, "I'll always remember Troy, Lily. I really cherish the table he made for me. It's absolutely beautiful craftsmanship."

Lily vividly remembered the piece of Troy's unfinished furniture still in storage. In fact, he'd been in the last stages of completing the plant stand she'd asked him to make when he was deployed. So much was unfinished and Lily didn't know how to complete the tapestry of the life that had been hers and Troy's.

Mitch had heard their conversation, too, and turned away, crossing to the refrigerator, closing the top on a juice bottle and setting it inside. His actions were slow and deliberate. She knew she'd brought up Troy to put a boundary around herself again, a boundary that would keep Mitch out. Why had she dropped in today? To catch up with old friends? Or to see *him?*

As Hillary moved away, rocking Sophie and cooing to her, Lily's gaze landed on Ellie, who was glancing toward her and then Mitch. No one else seemed to notice the vibes between Lily and Mitch, but apparently Ellie did.

Lily hung out with her colleagues in the lounge for a while. They all wanted to take turns holding the twins and see if they could distinguish between the two. As Lily had suspected, Hillary asked Ellie to tell her all about the clothes she created.

Stepping away from the group with Grace in her arms, Lily went in search of Mitch. He was her friend, and they would be working together when she returned. She had to keep communication open between them. She had to know what was going on in his mind. Maybe it had nothing to do with her. If it didn't, she'd be relieved. At least that's what she told herself.

She found him in his office, at his computer. She stood there for a few moments, listening to Grace's little soughing sounds, studying Mitch's profile. Her gaze went to his hands as his fingers depressed keys. His left hand was faster than his right and she wondered if the fingers on his right hand hurt to use. What kind of pain did he experience on a daily basis? With what he'd told her, she guessed his injuries had left repercussions. On the other hand, were the memories in his head more painful than anything physical injuries could cause? She wished he could talk to her about all of it. She wished—

Moving into the room, she said, "You should still be on your lunch break."

"A fertility specialist never sleeps," he joked. "I have a couple coming in this afternoon because the time is right."

"They're going the artificial insemination route?"

"For now. In vitro doesn't fit into their budget." His gaze went from Lily to Grace. "She seems content."

Lily checked her watch. "Probably for about fifteen more minutes."

Rolling his chair back, Mitch stood and approached her. His large hand gently passed over Grace's little head, his thumb brushing her strands of cotton-soft blond hair. "So you just decided to stop in or did you and Ellie have errands in the area?"

"Sophie and Grace had appointments with Tessa. Since we were in the building..." She trailed off.

"You wanted to stay in touch."

"I think it will be easier for me to come back to work in the fall if I do."

He nodded.

"Mitch..." She didn't know what she wanted to say, or how to say it. "I need to talk about Troy."

"I know you do. That was another good reason for Ellie coming to stay with you."

"You left the lounge and I thought—"

"I told you I have clients coming."

"I know." She felt so stymied for the right words to

say. She could say, *I want to be around you, but when I am, I feel guilty.* Yet that couldn't come out because she and Mitch were both fighting becoming any closer.

She bowed her head, placing a tiny kiss on Grace's forehead, trying to figure out what she was doing in this room with Mitch and why she had actually stopped in today.

Yet Mitch wouldn't let her stand there, stewing in her own confusion. He slipped one knuckle under her chin and lifted it. "I think we're both feeling things we don't believe we should be feeling. You don't know whether to run in the other direction or pretend we're just friends."

"I don't want to pretend!"

His brows arched as he gave her a crooked smile. "That *is* the crux of it."

"Lily." Ellie was standing in the doorway with Sophie, studying the two of them standing close, Mitch's finger under her chin.

He quickly dropped his hand to his side while Lily turned to face her sister-in-law. "I know. They're both going to start crying for lunch soon."

"If you'd like to use my office, you can," Mitch offered. "I have work to do in the lab."

Crossing to his desk and reaching for a file folder, he picked it up, then stopped in the doorway. "It's good to see you again, Ellie."

"You, too," she said politely.

Mitch stood there for a few moments as if waiting to see if Troy's sister had something else to say. But she didn't. After a last glance at Lily and the twins, he strode down the hall.

Lily waited, not knowing if Ellie might have something to say to *her*. But her sister-in-law just moved toward the door. "I'll get the diaper bag." Then she was gone, too, leaving Lily with Grace in Mitch's office with very chaotic thoughts and feelings.

"They sure like those swings," Angie observed a week later as Lily came into the kitchen and watched her putting together a casserole for lunch.

Lily stirred the white sauce she was cooking and glanced over at her content daughters. "They're settling into a real schedule."

"Where's Ellie?"

"She went shopping to get material she needed."

Angie poured herself a cup of coffee and took a seat at the kitchen counter. "Mitch hasn't been around for a while. Did you two have a fight or something?"

Or something, Lily thought. "I saw him when I visited everyone at the practice."

"That was a week ago. He stopped in to see Sophie and Grace every day when they were in the hospital and he worried about you. It seems odd he hasn't called or dropped by more."

"I think he's giving me space."

Angie studied Lily over her mug. "Do you want space?"

"We're just friends." If she repeated those words often enough, she might believe them.

"I know that. And I know he's watching over you because Troy asked him to."

Lily found herself wanting to protest, to say that wasn't the only reason. Yet she wasn't sure she should. She didn't know what was in Mitch's mind. "I feel I owe him so much for everything."

"So why not call him and ask him to dinner?"

Angie made it sound so simple. On the one hand, Lily would love to do that. But on the other, she wished she and Mitch could have a little time alone, maybe straighten out everything between them.

"I could go to his place to cook dinner," she said aloud, testing the idea.

From the doorway, several bags in her arms, Ellie asked, "You want to cook dinner for Mitch?" There was wariness in her tone and an element of disapproval.

"He did so much for me, including encouraging me to call you. I'd like to thank him."

Ellie came into the kitchen and dropped her bags on the table. Then she went to the twins and crouched down, greeting both of them.

"I'm off for the weekend," Angie offered. "I could watch Sophie and Grace if Ellie has plans."

"No plans tomorrow. Just the concert with you in Amarillo on Saturday," Ellie said to Angie, without looking up. "I can watch them."

"Are you sure?" Lily asked. "Because I could invite Mitch here instead."

"No," Ellie responded, standing. "It's fine. Angie and I and Sophie and Grace will have a girls' night together. It will be a blast, even if the babies can't eat popcorn yet."

"Before we make too many plans, I'd better find out if Mitch wants me to cook for him. I'll leave a message on his cell phone." She picked up the cordless phone in the kitchen before she lost her nerve.

An hour and a half later, when Mitch returned her call, Lily had just finished breast-feeding both babies.

It was much easier now than when she'd first tried to juggle their needs.

"I got your message," Mitch said. "Is everything all right?"

Lily looked down at her sleeping daughters. "Everything's fine. I…" She cleared her throat. "If you're going to be home tomorrow evening, I'd like to cook you dinner."

"Home? As in at my house?"

She laughed. "Yes. Angie and Ellie offered to watch Sophie and Grace, and this would be my way to thank you for everything you've done."

He didn't say, "You don't have to thank me," because they'd gone through that routine before and he probably knew it would fall on deaf ears. "A home-cooked meal would be a nice change," he agreed noncommittally.

"What's your favorite meal?"

"Why don't you surprise me."

"You're not going to give me a hint?"

"Nope. I like everything."

"Okay, I'll stop at the market and then come over."

"I'm taking off tomorrow afternoon to meet with the couple who own the bed-and-breakfast around three. But I should be home by four. I can tape a spare key under the garage spout in case I'm tied up longer."

Lily was surprised Mitch was taking off, but she knew planning the reunion was important to him. "That's perfect. I can get started and then when you arrive, we can really catch up."

"Catching up sounds good," he responded, as if he meant it.

Lily's heart seemed to flutter but she told herself it was just her imagination.

After she ended the call, she wondered if she was doing the right thing. But showing her appreciation was important to her. No matter what Mitch said, she believed it was important to him, too.

She'd find out tomorrow night.

Lily found the key behind the spout on Friday and let herself into Mitch's brick ranch-style house situated on the outskirts of Sagebrush. She liked the looks of the outside with its neat plantings and tall fencing, and the protected entrance where she'd set the grocery bags on a wooden bench that perfectly fit the space. Slipping the key into the lock, she pushed open the door and stepped inside.

To the right of the small foyer, a door led into the garage. Beyond that lay a rambling living room. It was huge, with a fireplace, tall windows and a cathedral ceiling with a fan. The comfortable-looking furniture was upholstered in masculine colors, navy and burgundy. Distressed-pine tables and black wrought-iron lamps sat in practical positions around the furniture. She was surprised to see only a small flat-screen TV in the entertainment center rather than a larger model. But then maybe Mitch didn't spend much time watching TV.

The kitchen was straight ahead and she eagerly picked up the bags, took them in and set them on the counter. Stainless steel appliances looked shiny and new. An archway opened into a sunroom where French doors led outside to a large rustic brick patio. A round table and four chairs nestled in a corner of the dining area of the kitchen under a black wrought-iron chandelier. She liked the clean lines of the house, its spaciousness, its practical floor plan.

She was unpacking the groceries when her cell phone rang. She thought it might be Mitch telling her he was on his way. Instead, she recognized Raina's number and happily answered. "How are you?"

Her friend said, "I'm in labor!"

"You're not due till next week," Lily said practically.

Raina laughed. "Tell that to our son or daughter."

"Where are you?"

"At the hospital. Emily is with me."

Lily knew Raina was comfortable using a midwife, but her husband hadn't been so sure. "How is Shep handling this?"

"Let's just say he drove here under the speed limit but that was a struggle. Now he's pacing while Emily's trying to keep the mood relaxed."

Raina had wanted to have a home birth, but she'd compromised with Shep. Since Emily and Jared had managed to bring about changes at the hospital to include a midwife in the birthing process, there were two suites there now that were supposed to simulate the comforts of home. The birthing suites provided the advantages of delivering a baby in a more natural setting while having a doctor nearby should any complications arise.

"How are *you* handling labor?"

"I can't wait for this baby to be born. Wow," she suddenly exclaimed, "I'm starting another contraction and it's stronger than the last one. Either Shep or I will let you know when the baby's born. Talk to you later."

Lily thought about her own contractions, how they'd come on so suddenly, how Mitch had helped her. In some ways, that night seemed eons ago.

After considering her options, Lily had decided to make Mitch something she had never cooked before. She'd found the recipe for chicken in wine in her favorite cookbook. It wasn't complicated. It just required a little time to prepare. Today she had the time. She'd brought along her favorite pan and started bacon frying in it. Rummaging in Mitch's cupboard, she found other pots and pans she could use. After she sorted her ingredients, she prepared the chicken to fry in the bacon drippings.

A half hour later, the chicken was browning nicely when she heard the garage door open. She took a quick look around the kitchen. She had managed to set the table before she'd started the chicken. She'd brought along two place mats, matching napkins, as well as a vase filled with pretty, hand-carved wooden flowers. Mitch's white ironstone dishes looked perfect on the dark green place mats.

Lily heard the door from the garage into the foyer open then Mitch's deep voice calling into the kitchen. "Something smells great."

And then he was there in the doorway, tall and lean, his almost black eyes taking in everything at a glance. He wore blue jeans, black boots and a navy henley. Skitters of sensation rippled up and down her spine.

They just stood there for a few moments, staring at each other. He assessed her white jeans and pink top with its scoop neckline. "Shouldn't you be wearing an apron?"

"The clothes will wash."

"Spoken like a mom."

Moving forward into the kitchen, he caught sight

of the table and stopped. "You've gone to a lot of trouble."

"Not really. You're just not used to a woman's touch." As soon as the words were out, she knew she should have thought first before speaking. Letting the thoughts in her mind spill free could land her in deep trouble.

Mitch didn't react, simply hung his keys on a hook above the light switch. "I don't know how long it's been since I walked into a kitchen with something good cooking. Do you want me to help with this?" He motioned to the stove and the sink. "Or do you want me to get out of your way?"

"You're welcome to help, but if you have something more important to do—"

"Nothing that can't wait," he said, washing his hands. "I worked in the yard earlier this afternoon."

"I like your house, and the way you've decorated."

His brows drew together as he dried his hands on the dish towel. "Maybe you can tell me the best way to set it up to entertain twenty to twenty-five people for the reunion weekend. I'm afraid space will be tight."

"What about a fire pit on the patio, depending on the weather, of course. It might draw a few people out there to toast marshmallows."

He studied her with one of those intense looks again and she knew it wasn't just the heat from the stove that was making her cheeks flame. "What?"

"You have great ideas."

Smiling to herself, she turned back to the chicken, deciding it was browned just right and that she had to concentrate on the meal so she wouldn't focus too much on Mitch. "My next great idea is that I'd better watch what I'm doing or your kitchen could go up in flames."

He chuckled. "What do you need help with?"

"Can you open the wine? I need a cup. I have everything else ready to simmer." She dumped in onions and celery, stirring to sauté them a bit, added carrots, chicken broth and the crumbled bacon. After Mitch loosened the cork and poured out a cup of wine, she took it from him, their hands grazing each other, hers tingling after they did.

Moving away from him, she poured the wine into the pot, put the lid on and set it to simmer, glad the major part of the meal was finished.

"Now what?" he asked.

"I need three apples peeled and sliced into that pie plate. I'll make the topping while you're doing that. Tell me about your meeting. Will you be able to reserve rooms at the bed-and-breakfast?"

When Mitch didn't answer, she looked up at him and saw him staring down at the apples. At that moment, she realized the request she'd made, as well as the mistake of asking him to do that kind of task.

"I've learned to do a lot of things with my left hand," he said matter-of-factly, "but using a knife to slice apples isn't one of them."

"Mitch, I'm sorry. I wasn't thinking."

"There's nothing to be sorry about. Why don't I look through my collection of DVDs and find something we would both enjoy?"

She wanted to put her arms around Mitch. She wanted to breathe in his scent and kiss him, letting him know the use of his fingers wasn't an issue between them.

"Okay," she said lightly. "I'll be there in a few

minutes." That was all the time she'd need to slice the apples, mix them with cranberries and pour on a topping.

Then she might have to decide just where she stood where Mitch was concerned.

Chapter Seven

Mitch knew he shouldn't have reacted as he had. It had been a very long time since something so simple had pushed his buttons. After Iraq, he'd been grateful he'd survived. He'd been grateful he could retrain in another specialty. He'd been grateful he had a life.

The truth was, he could have peeled an apple with his left hand, but those slices would have been chunky and choppy, maybe still bearing some skin.

At the practice, he spoke with couples, analyzed their needs, helped them decide which process was best. He calculated cycles, administered drug regimens, analyzed test results, sonograms, fluoroscopic X-rays. He could facilitate artificial insemination procedures. But he couldn't peel and slice an apple to his liking.

He could help bring life into the world, but he couldn't perform surgery to save a life.

Why had that fact hit him so hard just now?

He shuffled through the DVDs lying on the coffee table without paying attention to the titles. He was vaguely aware of the scent of cinnamon and apples baking, adding to the aroma of the chicken and wine. But when Lily stood in the doorway for a couple of moments before she took a step into the living room, he was elementally aware of her.

As she sat beside him on the sofa, only a few inches away, he wanted to both push her away and take her into his arms. It was the oddest feeling he'd ever experienced. Desire bit at him and he fought it.

"Dinner will be ready in about twenty minutes," she said, as if that were the main topic for discussion.

He could feel her gaze on him, making him hot, making him more restless. Facing her, he concluded, "Maybe this wasn't such a good idea."

"Eating dinner?" she asked, a little nervously, trying to make light of what was happening.

"Cooking together, eating together, watching a DVD together."

"I want to be here," she assured him, her eyes big and wide, all attempts at teasing gone. It was as if she were inviting him to kiss her.

He balled his hands into fists. "Lily—"

Reaching out to him, she touched the tense line of his jaw. "I don't know what's happening, Mitch, but being here with you is important to me. Maybe that first kiss wasn't as intense as we both thought it was. Maybe it was just an outlet—"

He was tired of analyzing and debating and pushing away desire that needed to be expressed. His hands slid under her hair as he leaned toward her, as he cut off her words with his lips. For over two years, he'd kept his desire for her hidden, locked away. Now, unable to resist, he set it free.

Passion poured out. Lily responded to it and returned it. For that reason, and that reason only, he didn't slam the door shut. He didn't throw the combination away again. She was softness and goodness and light in his hands. When his tongue swept her mouth, she wrapped her arms around his neck and held on. He was caught in the storm that had been building between them since the day he'd first held her. Warning bells clanged in his head, reminding him he should stop kissing her and pull away. But those warning bells seemed distant compared to the hunger that urged him on.

He sensed that same hunger had built in Lily. She wasn't holding back. Nothing about her was restrained.

The sounds of satisfaction Lily was making were driving Mitch crazy. His hand slid from her hair and caressed her shoulder. He could feel the heat of her skin under her knit top. Was she on fire for him as he was for her? Would she consider this kiss another mistake?

His hand slid to her breast. He knew if he didn't breathe soon, the need inside him would consume him.

Lily leaned away just slightly, as if inviting him to touch her more. His control was in shreds. He tore away from the kiss to nuzzle her neck as his hand left her breast and caressed her thigh.

When she turned her face up to his again, her eyes were closed. At that moment, Mitch knew this could be a very big mistake. What if she was imagining Troy loving her? What if she just needed someone to hold her and any man would take the form of her husband?

He leaned back, willed his heart to slow and found his voice. "Lily, open your eyes."

The few seconds it took for Lily to find her way back to the sofa seemed unending. She'd been so lost in pleasure that the sound of Mitch's voice—the request he'd made—seemed impossible at first.

When she did open her eyes, she was gazing into his. They were so dark and simmering, filled with the questions that took her a moment to understand. Until he asked, "Were you here with me?"

Her reflexive response was, "Of course, I was here with you." But as soon as she said it, she had to go back and think and feel. She had to be honest with Mitch and herself. As he didn't move an inch, she whispered, "*Mostly* here with you."

While she was kissing Mitch, had she been longing for Troy to be the one making love to her? Shaken by that question, as well as the aftermath of the passion that had bubbled up inside her like a well waiting to be sprung, she jumped when the cell phone in her pocket chimed.

Mitch seemed just as jarred. The resigned look on his face told her he knew she had to take the call. After all, Sophie or Grace might need her.

She checked the screen and then glanced at him. "It's Raina. She's in the hospital in labor. I have to find out if everything's okay."

Just then, the timer went off in the kitchen. Mitch rose to his feet. "I'll check on dinner," he said gruffly.

Lily closed her eyes and answered Raina's call.

Swallowing emotion that was confusing and

FREE Merchandise is 'in the Cards' for you!

Dear Reader,

We're giving away FREE MERCHANDISE!

Seriously, we'd like to reward you for reading this novel by giving you **FREE MERCHANDISE** worth over **$20**. And no purchase is necessary!

You see the Jack of Hearts sticker above? Paste that sticker in the box on the Free Merchandise Voucher inside. Return the Voucher promptly...and we'll send you valuable Free Merchandise!

Thanks again for reading one of our novels—and enjoy your Free Merchandise with our compliments!

Pam Powers

Pam Powers

P.S. Look inside to see what Free Merchandise is **"in the cards"** for you!

(S-SE-12/10)

W e'd like to send you two free books to introduce you to the Silhouette Special Edition® series. These books are worth over $10, but they are yours to keep absolutely FREE! We'll even send you 2 wonderful surprise gifts. You can't lose!

REMEMBER: Your Free Merchandise, consisting of **2 Free Books** and **2 Free Gifts**, is worth over $20.00! No purchase is necessary, so please send for your Free Merchandise today.

YOUR FREE MERCHANDISE INCLUDES...

2 FREE Silhouette Special Edition® Books

AND 2 FREE Mystery Gifts

FREE MERCHANDISE VOUCHER

2 FREE BOOKS and **2 FREE GIFTS**

Please send my Free Merchandise, consisting of
2 Free Books and **2 Free Mystery Gifts**.
I understand that I am under no obligation to buy
anything, as explained on the back of this card.

*About how many NEW paperback fiction books
have you purchased in the past 3 months?*

❏ 0-2   ❏ 3-6   ❏ 7 or more
E9EY   E9FC   E9FN

235/335 SDL

Please Print

FIRST NAME

LAST NAME

ADDRESS

APT.#   CITY

STATE/PROV.   ZIP/POSTAL CODE

NO PURCHASE NECESSARY!

▲ If offer card is missing write to: The Reader Service, P.O. Box 1867, Buffalo, NY 14240-1867 or visit www.ReaderService.com ▲

BUSINESS REPLY MAIL
FIRST-CLASS MAIL   PERMIT NO. 717   BUFFALO, NY

POSTAGE WILL BE PAID BY ADDRESSEE

THE READER SERVICE
PO BOX 1867
BUFFALO NY 14240-9952

NO POSTAGE
NECESSARY
IF MAILED
IN THE
UNITED STATES

exhilarating, as well as terrifying, Lily cleared her throat. "Raina?"

"It's a girl, Lily! We had a *girl*." Her friend's voice broke.

"That was pretty fast."

"Once we got here, it was like she couldn't wait to get out. You've got to come see her, Lily. I know you... understand."

Lily did understand Raina's history, the loss of her husband and dreams unfulfilled. Now she'd captured those dreams again. "I'm at Mitch's."

Raina didn't miss a beat. Her joy was too big and broad. "Bring him, too. Shep could use a little distraction. He's hovering over both of us. Eva's here with the boys but she's going to leave in a few minutes. They're so excited about their new sister that they're getting a little rowdy."

"I'll call you back after I talk to Mitch."

"If I interrupted something, I'm sorry. You can wait to visit tomorrow."

Yes, she could. Yet she knew the joy Raina was feeling. She knew this was a once-in-a-lifetime experience for her.

After she and Raina ended the call, Lily went into the kitchen, where Mitch had taken the apple dessert from the oven and set it on the counter.

"Raina had a baby girl," she announced brightly.

"I bet she and Shep are ecstatic."

She remembered Mitch had met Shep the night of the awards dinner that now seemed forever ago. "She'd like us to come see the baby."

"Now? She wants company?"

"You know how it is with new moms. They're so

proud, so full of life. And Raina and I, we have a special bond. She says we can wait until tomorrow, but I don't want to let her down. The chicken should be finished. Do you want to have dinner first?"

Mitch glanced at the kitchen clock. "Visiting hours will be over soon. Let's put it in a casserole. We can warm it up when we get back."

"I can go alone."

"Would you rather go alone?"

Their intimacy on the sofa was still fresh in her mind and in her heart. She wanted to stay with him...*be* with him a little longer.

"I'd like you to come along."

He gave her a hint of a smile. "Then let's put this away and get going."

Lily thought she'd jump out of her skin every time Mitch glanced at her in his SUV. Their awareness of each other was so acute, it was almost uncanny. She suspected Mitch was feeling the same way when he flipped on the CD player. Both of them had agreed to go to the hospital because that was the easier thing to do. She'd almost gotten naked with Mitch, almost let him make love to her. Then what would they have had to say to each other?

At the hospital, alone in the elevator as they rode up to the maternity floor, Mitch turned to her. "I don't feel as if I belong here."

"Here?"

"The maternity floor. With your friend."

"My guess is Shep will be glad to see a friendly male face. He's not real comfortable with the softer things in life, if you know what I mean. But I think Raina's changing that."

"Softer things in life, meaning women having babies, pink blankets, nurses cooing?"

"You've got it."

Mitch almost smiled. "That does take some getting used to."

"I guess the transition from trauma surgeon to fertility specialist wasn't always easy for you."

"Fortunately I was able to rely on some of the research skills I'd acquired while I was in med school. I was a teaching assistant for a professor studying T cells, so analyzing data and studies wasn't foreign to me. I think the hardest part was learning to act as a counselor sometimes to couples who were stressed out because they'd been trying for years to have a baby and couldn't. All kinds of things popped up. I suppose that's why we have Dr. Flannagan as an adjunct."

"Vanessa is good. I've sent couples to her who are indecisive or who can't agree on what they want to do. Do you know Vanessa well?" Lily asked.

"No. We had lunch together once to discuss a case. She doesn't like to skate on the surface and I didn't want to be psychoanalyzed, so let's just say we didn't socialize after that—we stuck to business."

Lily was surprised to find herself relieved that Mitch hadn't gotten on well with the pretty psychologist. She admonished herself that she had no business being possessive. She had *no* rights where Mitch was concerned.

After Lily and Mitch signed in at the desk, Lily caught sight of Shep in one of the family waiting rooms. Joey and Roy, Shep and Raina's older boys, stood in the doorway as if ready to leave. Eva, their nanny, had one arm about each of them while Manuel, Shep and

Raina's almost three-year-old, was throwing a tantrum, his arms tightly holding Shep around the neck, his tears as heartbreaking as his sobs.

"Daddy, you come home, *too,*" he wailed.

Shep spotted Lily immediately and said above Manuel's wails, "Don't you tell Raina about this."

"She'd understand."

"Hell, yes, she'd understand. She'd want me to bring them all into the room so they could sleep with her."

Lily had to chuckle because she knew Shep was right. "She'd call it a birthday sleepover," Lily joked.

Mitch groaned. "I think you're going to have to do better than that to cheer this little guy up. So your name's Manuel?" Mitch asked, bending down to him, looking into his eyes.

At first Lily thought the little boy would play shy. Instead of hiding in Shep's shoulder, though, he pulled himself up straighter and studied Mitch. "What's your name?"

"My name's Mitch." He pointed to Lily. "You know her, don't you?"

Manuel nodded vigorously. "She and Mom are BFFs."

The adults all looked at each other and broke out into laughter.

"Who'd you hear that from?" Shep asked.

"Joey. He knows."

"Yes, he does know lots of things," Shep agreed with a grin he couldn't suppress.

"Maybe you should go home and make sure everything's ready for tomorrow when your sister comes home," Mitch suggested. "I bet your mom and dad would both be surprised."

Eva stepped in. "We could cut some roses and put them in pretty vases. Your mom would love that. We can make sure everything in the baby's room is just right."

Manuel stared at Eva.

Adding another incentive, she offered, "I can turn on the new baby monitor and you can watch the lights flicker when we make noise in the room."

Swiveling toward his dad again, Manuel screwed up his little face. "Okay."

Shep tapped the pocket of his shirt. "I'll give you a call before bed and you can say good-night to Mom. How's that?"

"That's good," Manuel assured him, climbing off his dad's lap and taking Eva's hand.

After hugs and kisses from all his boys, Shep watched them leave the maternity floor with Eva.

"Man, that's tough," he muttered. "It breaks my heart when they're sad."

Lily patted Shep's arm knowing that before he met Raina, he never would have been able to admit that.

"I'm going to visit the new mom," Lily said.

Shep studied Mitch. "You want to get a cup of coffee with me?"

"Sure," Mitch answered, exchanging a look with Lily that told her she'd been right about Shep needing a break.

"See you in a bit," she said with a wave, and headed for Raina's room.

When she entered her friend's room, she stopped short. This was a woman who had her world together.

The head of the bed had been raised and Raina was holding her infant daughter. She looked absolutely radiant and Lily almost envied her calm sense of satisfaction.

"Hey, there," she called softly from the doorway.

"Hey, yourself. Come on in. Meet Christina Joy McGraw."

"What a beautiful name! Did you and Shep decide on it together?"

"He just said he wanted something pretty and a little old-fashioned. I added Joy because that's what she's going to bring us." After passing her hand over her baby's head, Raina looked beyond Lily. "Where's Mitch?"

"He's keeping Shep company for a cup of coffee."

"This is a rough day for Shep, but if he drinks more than two cups, he's not going to sleep tonight."

Lily laughed. "I don't think he's going to sleep anyway. You *do* know he's going to stay here with you."

"He said something to that effect, but I thought he was kidding."

"Uh-uh. He's not letting you or that baby girl out of his sight for very long."

After they both stared down at the infant, Lily taken with her raven-dark hair and eyes, Raina asked, "Did I interrupt something when I called? I never imagined you'd be with Mitch."

"Oh, I just decided to make him a thank-you dinner. It was easier to do at his house."

"Did you eat?"

"No, we put it in a casserole for later. It will be fine."

"I have lousy timing," Raina murmured.

"No, actually you have very good timing."

The two women exchanged a look.

"Do you want to tell me what's going on?" Raina asked.

"Not here. The men could come back. Besides, I'm not sure anything is going on. Nothing should be going on, right?" If there was one person to ask about this, that person would be Raina.

"I waited nine long years to find love again. You don't have to wait that long."

"But what if it isn't love? What if I just miss Troy so much, long to be held so much, that I mistake something else for real emotion?"

"Is that what you think is happening?"

Lily sighed. "I don't know. When I'm with Mitch, I actually can't think sometimes, let alone figure out the best thing to do."

"Then don't do anything until you're ready to do whatever's right for you."

"You make it sound so easy."

"Yeah, I know," Raina said with a wry smile. "If I'd taken my own advice, I wouldn't have this little girl in my arms right now. Do you want to hold her?"

"You bet I do."

Shep sat across from Mitch at the cafeteria table, staring down into his coffee. "When Raina went into labor—" He shook his head. "I don't think I've ever gone into such a panic."

"I know what you mean," Mitch said, thinking about that night at the banquet, Lily's contractions, knowing the twins would be premature.

Shep didn't say anything for a moment, but then remarked, "So you felt that way when Lily went into labor?"

What kind of trap had Mitch just walked into? He kept silent.

"You being a doc and all," Shep went on, "I would think you'd be more matter-of-fact about it."

He would have been with anyone else, but not with Lily. No way was he going to admit that out loud. Then it didn't seem he had to. Shep was giving him a knowing look that made Mitch feel uncomfortable. One thing Mitch never thought he'd be was transparent. He expected another question, but it didn't follow.

Instead, Shep took another sip of his coffee and set it down again. "Raina and Lily have become really good friends. They have a lot in common."

"Raina's been a great support for Lily since Troy died." He might as well just get the subject out there so they weren't trampling around it.

"I heard you've been, too."

"You heard?" Mitch tried to keep the defensiveness from his voice, but he was worried that gossip was spreading about him and Lily.

"That night at the banquet when you carried Lily off. Raina told me Troy had left a letter asking you to look after her. That's why you're with her again tonight, right?" Shep inquired blandly.

Lily had told Mitch about Shep's background and why he'd wanted to adopt. She'd always spoken admiringly of him and Mitch knew her to be a good judge of character.

So when Shep stopped beating around the proverbial bush and added, "When I met Raina, nine years had passed since her husband died. Even so, we had a few bumps in our road because of it."

"Lily and I aren't—"

"Aren't serious? Aren't involved? Only friends? I get that. No one's judging you...or Lily."

"Maybe *you're* not, but Troy's sister is and I can't blame her for that. Even *I* know Lily's still vulnerable and I should watch my step. But how do you keep a promise to protect someone and step back at the same time?"

"That's a tough one," Shep admitted. "But if you care about her, you'll figure out the right thing to do, without interference from anyone else." Shep drank the last of his coffee. "Thanks for coming down here with me. I want to be with my wife and baby, but I needed a little break just to settle down a bit."

"I understand."

Shep nodded. "So are you ready to meet my daughter?"

When Lily and Mitch returned from the hospital, they warmed up dinner and ate at the table Lily had set. She called Ellie to see how the twins were doing and to give a report on Raina.

After she closed her phone, Mitch asked, "Ready for dessert?" and brought the apple crumble to the table.

"I have to get back home. Sophie and Grace are okay but I don't want Ellie and Angie to feel as if I've abandoned them."

"You haven't. A couple of hours away will do all of you good."

"I know, but—"

"You don't have to run off because you think I might kiss you again. I won't, if you don't want me to."

Lily felt her heart start hammering. "That's the problem, Mitch. I think I want you to."

Although another man might have acted on that subtle invitation, Mitch didn't. He set the dish on the table and started scooping dessert out for both of them.

"You don't have anything to say to that?" she asked quietly.

"Shep thinks we're involved."

Lily felt rattled that the subject had come up between the two men.

"I didn't start that conversation, if you're wondering," Mitch assured her.

"No, I wasn't. I guess I was just surprised."

"Everyone who cares about you is worried about you. It's natural that they're going to watch what you're doing."

"I hate to think I'm being watched," Lily murmured.

"In a good way."

After Mitch took his seat again beside her, she confessed, "Raina thinks we're involved, too."

"And what do *you* think?" he asked, his dark gaze penetrating, assessing, questioning.

"I think I'm scared. I think a kiss means more than I want it to mean with you."

"We did more than kiss," he reminded her.

She couldn't look away, didn't look away, wouldn't look away. She had to be as honest as she could with him. "I'm not sure where we're headed, Mitch. A lot of hormones are still driving me. What if we go up in flames? How much damage will that do to either of us? I've never had affairs, even before Troy. I was always in committed relationships. So what's happening between you and me—"

"Isn't a committed relationship."

"We're really on sandy footing," she said with a shake of her head.

He didn't disagree.

"But I like being with you," she continued. "I feel so alone sometimes, but not when I'm with you."

"We're back to the friends-versus-more question," he said.

Suddenly Lily was tired of the seriousness of it all. She was a widow with two babies to raise and sometimes she just wanted to scream. "Why do we even have to decide? Why are we worried about affairs and committed relationships? I mean, why can't we just enjoy being together?"

A light smile crept across his lips. "You couldn't be saying we're analyzing too much."

"I'm saying I need to take some deep breaths and not worry so much, and maybe *you* do, too. Yes, I think about Troy all the time, and how much I miss him, and how much the babies would love to have him as a father. But he's not here, and I can't pretend he will be again."

"You still love him a lot."

"Yes, Mitch, I do. But that love can't fill up my life twenty-four hours a day anymore. I have to start making room for a different life."

"And?" Mitch prompted.

"And," Lily repeated, then hesitated a moment.... "And Ellie and Angie are going to a concert in Amarillo tomorrow. They're going to stay overnight. So why don't you come over around four and we'll take the babies for a walk. Then maybe we can toss around some ideas for your Christmas weekend. That will be looking ahead and it should be fun. I can plan a menu. You can decide who will be Santa Claus. We'll just hang out."

His gaze was still on her, seeing into her and through her. They had to both figure out what they wanted and maybe the only way to do that would be to spend some time together.

"You just want some help with Sophie and Grace," he teased.

After considering what he'd said, she shook her head. "No, I want to hang out with you."

If she thought Mitch had ignored her invitation earlier, she could see in his eyes now that he hadn't.

Leaning toward her, he reached out and moved a stray wave from her cheek. Then he rubbed his thumb over her lips, leaning even closer. "Does hanging out involve kissing?"

"Maybe," she said with a little uncertainty.

His lips came down on hers and the rest of the world fell away.

Chapter Eight

Mitch pushed the double stroller down the street, noticing the darkened gray sky and the storm clouds that had gathered. He felt a similar storm inside of himself, agitating to be set free.

We're just going to hang out together, he repeated in his mind like a mantra.

Strolling beside him, Lily bent to make sure Sophie and Grace were happy under their canopies. Lily wore a yellow sundress with strawberries appliquéd around the hem. He wondered if she'd dressed up for him or if he was reading too much into her choice of a simple dress on a warm June day. She'd tucked her hair behind her ears and held it in place with two pretty mother-of-pearl combs. She was a vision that plagued his dreams and unsettled his days.

When she straightened, she flashed him a quick smile. "You're staring."

"Caught in the act," he joked. "You look pretty today. But more than that. Freer somehow."

"It was nice being in the house alone with the babies the few hours before you came. Don't get me wrong. I'm so grateful for how Angie and Ellie help. I love being housemates with them. But I also like the feeling that I'm Sophie and Grace's mother and no one means as much to them as I do. Isn't that silly?"

"Not at all. But you don't have to worry. Their eyes are starting to follow you. They know you're their mother, no matter who takes care of them. You have an innate bond with them, just as they do with each other. Nothing will change that."

"Not even me going back to work?"

"Not even."

The breeze suddenly picked up, tossing Lily's hair across her shoulders. "Uh-oh," she said, looking up. "We might not make it back before it rains."

"The rain could hold off," he assured her, yet he knew it probably wouldn't. Once the weather cycle was set in motion, nothing could stop it.

"I'm not wearing running shoes. *You* are."

"I promise I won't race ahead of you. Sophie and Grace are protected by the state-of-the-art stroller your friends gave them. So I don't think we have to rush on their part."

Still, he rolled the stroller around in a half circle and headed back the way they'd come.

Lily stepped up her pace beside him. "I don't like sudden storms."

"You'd rather have planned storms?" he asked, amused.

She cast him a sideways glance. "I know you think that's funny, but just imagine. What if you knew ahead of time about the crises in your life? You could prevent them."

"Maybe. Or maybe fate would just find another way to get you to the same spot so you'd have to make the same kind of decisions."

"Oh my gosh! You're a philosopher and I never knew it."

Mitch had to laugh. "That's one title I've never been given."

"It's a compliment," she assured him, with a teasing tone in her voice that made him want to tug her into his arms and kiss her right there and then on the street. But in Sagebrush, that would almost be a spectacle.

She must have guessed what he was thinking because she slowed for a moment. He didn't stop, and she took a couple of running steps to catch up.

The wind buffeted them with a little more force now and large, fat drops of rain began to pelt them. Lightning slashed the sky not so far away and thunder grumbled overhead. The flashes and booms reminded Mitch of faraway places. He fought to keep memories at bay. Even though he was practically jogging with the stroller, he took deep, even breaths, reminding himself where he was and what he was doing.

A half block from the Victorian, the rain became steadier, rat-a-tatting on the pavement, pelting the leaves of the Texas ash trees blurred in Mitch's peripheral vision. The thunder became a louder drumroll.

Mitch blocked the sound as best he could.

Almost at the front yard of the big, blue house with its yellow gingerbread trim, Lily's sandal caught on the uneven pavement. Mitch sensed rather than saw what was happening and training took over. He reached low for Lily, catching her around the waist before she fell. Her body was warm, her shoulders slick with the rain dripping down. One of her arms had surrounded his waist as she'd steadied herself to keep from falling. His face was so close to hers he could almost feel the quiver of her chin as emotion and desire ran through them both.

Yet they seemed to recognize where they were and what they were doing at the same time because in unison, they murmured, "The twins."

Mitch tilted his forehead against hers for just a moment then released her and pushed the stroller up the walkway to the porch.

Lily unlocked the door while he easily lifted the stroller, carrying it up the steps and into the foyer.

Moments later she switched on the Tiffany light to dispel the shadows while he rolled the twins into the living room and stooped down at Sophie's side of the stroller to see if any pelts of rain had made their way to her.

Lily did the same on Grace's side. "They're dry," she said with amazement.

"At least their clothes are," he returned with a wink.

When Lily laughed, he felt as if he'd done something terrific. He also felt as if the lightning strike had sent supercharged awareness through *him*. When his eyes met Lily's, he knew she felt the same way.

Ducking her head, she lifted Grace. Her pink-and-yellow playsuit with the dog appliquéd on her belly was a little big. It wouldn't be long until she grew into it, Mitch knew.

Grace cooed at Lily and Lily cooed back. "You're a happy girl today. How would you like to sit in your swing?"

Grace's little mouth rounded in an O and her very blue eyes studied her mom's face.

Mitch held Sophie in the crook of his arm. "Do you want to join your sister?"

Sophie's outfit was pink-and-green with a cat appliquéd on the bib of her overalls. When she waved her arms and oohed and aahed in her baby language, Mitch chuckled.

He and Lily set the girls in their swings and wound the mechanism that would start the motion. Then of one accord, she and Mitch seemed to come together, standing close behind the twins.

He brushed his hand down her arm. "I think you need a towel." She was wet from the rain and he was, too. The result of that seemed to be steam rising from both of them.

"I need to change," she murmured but didn't move away.

He fingered one of her combs. "I like these in your hair."

"They were my mother's," she replied softly. "I haven't worn them very much. I was afraid something would happen to them. Suddenly today I realized she wouldn't want me to just leave them in my jewelry box."

Lily's skin was lightly tanned as if she'd taken the babies for walks many days in the sun. He clasped her shoulders and ran his thumbs up and down the straps of her dress. "I've been wanting to kiss you since I got here."

"I've wanted you to kiss me since you got here."

She tilted her head up and he lowered his. He told himself to go easy, not to scare her with too much need. He didn't want to need her at all. But the moment his lips settled on hers, he couldn't keep the hunger at bay. The feel of her in his arms was exquisite, the soft pressure of her lips was a temptation that urged him to claim her. When his tongue thrust into her mouth, her gasp was only a preliminary response. She followed it with a tightening of her arms around him. A return taste of him became a chase and retreat that had them pressing their bodies together.

Outside, a bright flash of light against a darkening sky was soon followed by thunder that seemed to crawl up one side of the roof and down the other. The crackle and boom sounded very close.

All at once the light in the foyer went out and the hum of the refrigerator ceased.

Mitch held Lily tighter, ended the kiss and rubbed his jaw against her cheek. "The electricity." Huskiness hazed his words. "The lightning must have hit a transformer."

After a few moments, she leaned away from him. "I'd better find the oil lamp in case we don't have power for a while. I had a stir-fry planned for supper."

"We'll have to make do with lunchmeat and cheese."

"I made a coconut cake. We don't need power to eat that."

"You have flashlights and candles?"

"I think they're under the kitchen sink. The oil lamp's upstairs. I'll get it when I change."

"Go ahead. I'll watch Grace and Sophie until you come back down. Then you can stay with them while I rummage."

After a last longing look at him, sending the message their kiss had ended much too soon, she ran upstairs.

Mitch took a hefty breath.

Sandwiches eaten, candles and oil lamp lit, Lily forgot about time and just lived in the moment. She and Mitch had talked as they'd sat on the sofa and exchanged fussy babies. They'd played patty-cake and peekaboo with Sophie and Grace in between talking about books they had read, movies they'd seen, first experiences swimming, diving, surfing, hiking. There seemed to be so much to talk about. Yet underneath it all, whenever their gazes met or their fingers brushed, memories of their kisses danced in her mind.

After a few hours, Lily breast-fed Grace while Mitch bottle-fed Sophie. Sophie finished first, and he laid her in her crib, starting her mobile.

They'd brought the oil lamp to the babies' room while they fed them. A flameless candle Mitch had found in a cupboard glowed in place of a night-light. Shadows were heavy in the room and Lily could see Mitch caring for her daughter, gently making sure she was settled, watching her for a few moments, then touching his fingers to her forehead.

He would make a wonderful father.

Turning from the crib, he stooped to pick up the bottle he'd set on the floor. "I'll wash this out."

Grace had stopped suckling and her eyes were closed.

Lily raised her to her shoulder until she heard a little burp, and then she carried her to her crib, settling her in for the night, then she took the oil lamp to the bathroom where she set it on the vanity. A small candle burned next to the sink where Mitch was rinsing the bottle. He'd rolled up his shirtsleeves and for the first time, Lily saw the scars on his right forearm. She didn't look somewhere else, but studied the lines that still looked raw...the gashes that had healed but would never fade away.

Slowly she raised her eyes to his.

He turned off the spigot and blew out the candle.

He was about to roll down his sleeve when she stopped him, her hand clasping his. "You don't have to hide them from me."

"They're ugly."

"No, they're a badge of honor." Without thinking, only feeling, she bent and kissed one of the welts.

"Lily." He said her name in a way he never had before. His words were thick with need, with desire that needed to be expressed.

Her lips lingered on his skin for a few seconds, maybe because she wanted to anticipate what might happen next, maybe because she was afraid of what might happen next.

When she straightened, he took her face in both of his hands. "Do you know what you're doing?" he asked, his voice raspy.

"I'm feeling," she said without apology.

"Damn," he growled, wrapping his arms around her, possessing her lips with his.

His kiss was long and hungry, wet and wild. Lily felt like someone else, like a woman who could throw caution to the side and be free from the chains of what she should and shouldn't do. She kissed Mitch with a fervor that shocked her, yet gave her hope.

Lily's breasts pressed into Mitch's chest. Instead of trying to touch her with his hands, he let their bodies communicate. His breathing was as hot and heavy as hers. They fit together with perfect temptation, perfect anticipation, perfect exhilaration. He seemed to wait for some sign from her that she wanted more and she gave it, pressing even closer. She felt his hardness, the desire he'd been controlling up until now. There would be no turning back from this.

She didn't want to turn back. She wanted tonight with Mitch. Did he want her as badly? Would he let his scars be an issue?

She lowered her hand from his shoulder and insinuated it between their bodies, cupping him, leaving him with no doubt as to what she was ready to do.

Still holding her securely, Mitch backed her out of the bathroom…across the hall…into her bedroom. The area was pitch-black, the glow from the oil lamp in the bathroom the only light, reaching just inside the door. But that didn't stop them. The dark seemed to hold some comfort for them both. Once they were enveloped by it, their mouths sought each other, their arms embraced, their fingers touched. The dark held more excitement than anything else.

Mindlessly, Lily reached for Mitch's shirt buttons.

He searched for the edges of her top and somehow managed to pull it up and over her head.

After he'd tossed it, she asked, "Do you have a condom?"

His hands went still on her waist. "Yes, I do." He

reached into his pocket, pulled out the foil packet and dropped it on the nightstand.

They'd both known this night was coming, hadn't they?

"I'd hoped," Mitch said honestly. "That's why I brought it."

His hands slid to her bra and unhooked it. She shrugged off the straps quickly and leaned forward, kissing his chest. She couldn't see but she could feel hot skin against her lips. Her hands became her eyes as she ran them down his flat abdomen and stopped at the waistband of his jeans. His belt was pliant but fought her hands as she tried to unfasten it. He helped her with it. A few moments later, he'd shed his sneakers, jeans and briefs. She'd flicked off her sandals. Now he slid his hands into the waistband of her shorts, sliding them down her hips along with her panties.

She knew he couldn't see much more than shadows, either, and she asked, "Should I light a candle?"

"No time," he muttered as he pushed her hair aside and kissed her neck, trailing his lips along her collarbone. His foray to her breast made her restless, flushed and needy.

"Mitch," she moaned, but he didn't stop. He just kept kissing lower, down her belly to the mound between her thighs. She couldn't let him be that intimate. She just couldn't. The reason why eluded her.

She grasped his shoulders and said again, "Mitch."

This time she felt him shift, felt his head tilt up. He straightened, flung back the covers, and climbed into bed, holding his hand out to her.

Thunder grumbled again outside and she thought fleetingly of Grace and Sophie and whether or not they'd awaken. She listened as the sky rolled but heard nothing from the babies' bedroom.

As if he read her mind, Mitch asked, "Do you want to check on them?"

She knew she'd hear them if they awakened, even without the monitor. "They'll let us know if they wake up," she replied, crawling in beside him, moving closer to him.

He wrapped his arm around her and stroked her back. "You'll have to tell me what you like."

She suddenly couldn't speak and didn't know why. So she tilted her head against his and finally managed, "I want *you,* Mitch. Kiss me and everything else will be okay."

His lips were searingly hot, his tongue an instrument of pleasure that urged her to caress his back, his sides, his manhood.

"Lily," he gasped. "Are you ready?"

"Yes, Mitch. I am."

Reaching to the nightstand, he grabbed the packet and ripped open the foil. After he slid the condom on, he stretched out on top of her, letting her feel his weight. He spread her legs and lay between them. As he braced himself on his elbows, she tensed a little. He must have felt it because he kissed her again until all she wanted was him filling her, giving her pleasure, helping her to forget.

Forget what? a little voice inside her head whispered, but she ignored it, not bothering to find the answer.

When Mitch entered her, she *was* ready. Each of his thrusts made her call his name, asking for more. Mitch's body was as slick as hers with their passion. His chest slid against her breasts as they rocked, tempting each other, provoking each other to the next level of pleasure. Lily held on tightly as a strong orgasm overtook her, shaking her world until it was upside down. Mitch's shuddering release came moments later.

She felt as if the storm had somehow come inside. Stunned by the pleasure still tingling through her, she also felt overwhelmed by the intimacy she'd experienced with Mitch. She wobbled on the verge of feelings that terrified her and she didn't know whether to run or to hold on to Mitch for dear life.

After Mitch collapsed on top of her, he whispered in her ear, "Are you okay?"

She didn't know how to answer him, but gave him the response that would be easiest. "Yes, I'm good."

He kissed her cheek then rolled onto his side, taking her with him, their bodies still joined. "Do you want me to check on Sophie and Grace?"

"In a minute." She was still catching her breath, still trying to absorb what they had done, what she had done.

"Talk to me, Lily."

"Just hold me, Mitch. Just hold me."

"I shouldn't fall asleep with you. I could have a nightmare."

"It doesn't matter, I don't want you to leave."

So Mitch stayed and she held on, unsure what morning would bring.

Lily snuck glances at Mitch as they made breakfast the next morning. The night before, the first time the twins had awakened, Mitch had climbed out of bed quickly. Lily wondered if he'd slept at all because he'd seemed so wide awake as they fed Sophie and Grace and settled them once more. Afterward, Mitch had kissed her and she thought they might make love again. Instead he'd said, "Get some sleep. I'm going to bunk on the couch. When the electricity clicks back on, I'll make sure everything's working okay."

"Mitch, you could sleep with me."

But he'd shaken his head and she'd known better than to argue.

The twins had slept later than usual this morning, so it was almost ten o'clock as she scrambled eggs and Mitch fried bacon. Sophie and Grace faced each other and babbled in their swings.

She hadn't talked to Mitch about last night. They'd been too busy changing, dressing, diapering and now making breakfast. What she wanted to ask most was, *What did last night mean to you?*

However, as she was about to begin the discussion, the front door swung open and Angie and Ellie charged in, overnight cases in hand. They gave some attention to the babies and then stopped short when they saw Mitch.

Cheerfully, Angie tried to set the tone. "Good morning."

"I didn't expect you back so soon," Lily remarked. "How was the concert?"

"It was wonderful," Angie replied. "I felt like a teenager again. Brad Paisley is one hot dude."

Lily forced a laugh because Ellie was being so quiet.

Angie slipped a CD from her purse. "I got his new one."

"Did you have a good time?" she asked Ellie. Mitch silently listened, forking the slices of bacon.

"Yeah, it was great. But we heard you had storms last night and a lot of the electricity was out. We were worried. That's why we got up early and drove back. I tried to call but the phone must not be working. It just kept ringing and you didn't answer your cell, either."

"Oh, I'm sorry you worried," Lily apologized. "My cell was out of power when the electricity went down and I unplugged the charger so it wouldn't get damaged if there was a surge." She felt as if she were overexplaining and Ellie was eyeing her and then Mitch. Lily felt uncomfortable.

"Did you have any trouble getting back?" Mitch asked. "Trees down? That kind of thing?"

"Just a tree down on Alamo," Angie answered when Ellie didn't. "Branches here and there. We heard a tornado went through Odessa. That's why we were worried. How did Sophie and Grace do with the storm?"

"They didn't seem to mind," Mitch said with a smile.

"How long have you been here?" Ellie inquired.

Mitch looked to Lily, obviously deciding to let her answer. She felt suddenly unsettled, as if what had happened with Mitch last night was definitely all wrong. She was the mother of three-month-old twins. What was she doing having an affair? What was she doing making love with a man when Troy hadn't been gone a year? What was she doing trying to find a life when her old one still seemed so real?

Suddenly plagued by doubts, she answered, "Mitch came over last evening to visit. While he was here, the electricity went off. He stayed to make sure we were all safe. He slept on the couch and when the power came back on, he made sure everything was working right again."

She sensed Mitch's body tense. With a sideways glance at him, she saw his jaw set and his mouth tighten. She didn't dare look into his eyes.

"I see," Ellie responded.

Silence shrouded the kitchen until Angie broke it. "We bought donuts at the convenience store. I left them in the car with the souvenirs. I'll go get them."

"I can throw more eggs into the pan," Lily offered. "We have plenty of bacon and toast."

Mitch switched off the burner, fished the bacon from the pan and let it drain on a paper towel on a dish. But then he said, "I think I'll be going. Everything's back to normal here and the three of you can catch up."

Lily reached out a hand to him. "Mitch, you don't have to go."

His gaze locked to hers. "Yes, I think I do."

Lily felt her heart drop to her stomach. The look on Mitch's face told her that her explanation to Ellie hadn't been what he'd expected her to say. She slid the eggs from the pan onto a serving dish and set it on the table.

"I'll be right back," she told Ellie. "I'm going to walk Mitch out."

Mitch stopped by Sophie and Grace, jiggled their feet, gave them a last long look, then went to the living room. Making sure the timer on the swings would keep the babies content for a little while longer, Lily bent down and kissed them both. She passed Angie in the living room and saw that Mitch had already gone out the door.

"What's up?" Angie whispered to her.

"We'll talk later," she told her friend, not knowing what to expect when she went outside.

Lily had never seen Mitch angry. A sense of calm always seemed to surround him. But now, even though he was still, he wasn't calm. His brown eyes simmered with an emotion she didn't understand. She thought he was accusing her of something and she went on the defensive.

"You could stay for breakfast."

"If I stayed and Ellie asked what happened last night, what should I tell her?"

Maybe the emotion she was witnessing in Mitch's eyes wasn't anger. It was something worse. It was betrayal.

Her hands suddenly felt clammy. "I couldn't tell her what happened."

"I understand you want to keep your life private. I understand you're afraid you'll hurt her feelings. I understand that you feel she'd be upset if she thinks you're moving on. What I don't understand, especially after last night, is that you gave her the impression I was like a security guard seeing to your safety. Why are you afraid to admit to yourself what happened last night. We were *intimate*, Lily, as intimate as two people can be. Do you want to erase that from your memory?"

The breeze tossed her hair across her cheek as she self-consciously looked around to make sure no one was walking anywhere nearby. Glancing over her shoulder, she needed to be certain neither Angie nor Ellie were in the foyer, listening.

"I don't know what to think about last night," she admitted. "I'm not like that, Mitch. I don't seek pleasure to wipe out—"

"Loss and grief and memories?"

"Why are you so angry?"

He ran his hand over his face and considered her words carefully. "I don't think I'm as angry with you as I am with myself. I should have known better. I should have known you weren't ready."

She remembered him asking her last night, "Are you ready?" He'd meant so much more than the physical. Deep down, she'd known that.

"The dark made it easy," he decided. "The dark let you think, subconsciously at least, that you were with your husband again."

She wanted to protest. She wanted to scream that he was wrong. Yet how could she? She didn't know if he was wrong or right. She didn't know if last night had been about her and Mitch, or if it had been about her needing a man to hold her. She felt awful. She felt as if she *had* betrayed him.

"I'm going to leave before I say something else I shouldn't," he muttered. "It's probably better if we don't see each other for a while."

For a while? How long was that? She'd be going back to work in November. He didn't mean that long, did he? But she had her pride and he had his. She'd hurt him badly and now she had to suffer the consequences.

He took his car keys from his pocket. "Take care of yourself, Lily."

Moments later, he was driving down the street away from her.

Taking a deep, shaky breath, she tried not to think or feel and went inside to Grace and Sophie.

Chapter Nine

Late November

Lily sat across from Mitch in his office, hardly able to bear the awkwardness that had developed between them.

She'd been back at work for two weeks and had only caught glimpses of Mitch. He had definitely made himself scarce. The only reason they were in the same room together now was because they had to discuss a patient. "Joan Higgins has high levels of FSH, which definitely lowers the quality of her eggs. I think further testing is indicated."

Mitch nodded, keeping his gaze on the notes on his desk.

After he'd left the Victorian that morning in June, he'd emailed Lily every few weeks to inquire about her health and her daughters'. *Emailed*. He was doing his duty and keeping his promise to Troy without truly getting involved.

Could she blame him?

Lily desperately wanted to blurt out to Mitch, "I miss you," yet she knew she couldn't. She'd hurt him greatly by making love with him while she grieved for her husband. But he'd hurt *her* by walking away as he had. If he could leave her life so easily, what had that night meant to him? What if they'd continued the affair? Would he eventually have opened up to her? Would he have been ready to care for her and the twins out of more than duty?

"I'll order further tests," he agreed, ending their discussion of the patient.

They sat in awkward silence.

Finally Mitch laid down his pen. "How does it feel to be back at work?" His expression was neutral and he could have been making polite conversation with any of their colleagues.

"It feels good to be back. But I miss Sophie and Grace," she added honestly, as if he were still the old Mitch. "I miss not being able to hold them whenever I want. I mostly miss not hearing every new baby word first."

"You could come in part time," he suggested, as an employer might.

"I might be able to do that for a month or so, but I need my salary. I can't just think about the moment, I have to think about the future."

When their gazes collided, they were both thinking about taking pleasure in the moment, and the night neither of them would forget. At least, Lily hoped Mitch wouldn't forget it. She knew *she* never would.

Mitch pushed the papers on his desk into a stack, clipped them together and tossed them into his in-box. "It's getting late. I won't keep you any longer. I know you want to get home."

"Sophie and Grace are really growing and changing."

He looked surprised she'd started up the conversation again.

Reaching into her lab coat pocket, she drew out a small picture portfolio. "These are the latest pictures... if you'd like to see them. I can't believe they're already nine months old."

Maybe she was making it difficult for him to refuse to look, but right now she needed to see emotion from him, something more than a polite facade meant just for her. She'd ached for him all these months, but she hadn't been able to do more than answer his emails in the same tone he'd sent them—politely and with pertinent information. Yet seeing him and working with him again, she realized how much she'd lost when he'd walked away.

As she slid the little booklet across the desk to him, she confessed, "I need to keep their faces close by."

He stared at the small album for a couple of seconds and then picked it up. After he leafed through it, he stood and handed it back to her. "They're beautiful kids, Lily. I imagine in a few weeks, you'll have their picture taken with Santa Claus."

Yes, the holidays were coming and she found she didn't want to celebrate them without Mitch. Did he feel anything when he looked at Sophie and Grace's photos?

Did he wonder if the monitor was still working? If the sun rose and set now without her feeling grief twenty-four hours a day? What could she say to him to bring warmth back into his eyes?

She returned the photos to her pocket and rose to her feet. Obviously, he wanted her to leave. She could feel the figurative miles he was trying to shove between them. She'd let him do that for the past five months because she hadn't known what else to do, what was fair, what was necessary. But she couldn't merely leave things like this, emotions all tangled up, words gone unsaid, desires left unfulfilled.

"Mitch, what can I do to fix this?"

He didn't pretend to not know what she was talking about. "I don't think there's anything to fix."

It had taken courage on her part to bring it up, but he had shot her down without a glimmer of understanding...without a glimmer of hope that they could reestablish the connection they once had. She felt foolish and embarrassed. She should just go home to the people who loved her and wipe from her memories everything that had happened with Mitch.

She'd almost reached the door when she felt his hand on her shoulder. That simple touch brought back everything—the long, wet kisses, his hands on her body, the orgasm that had swept her to another realm. She hoped the naked feelings weren't showing in her eyes.

"I don't know how to fix it," he admitted. "We crossed the line and we can't go back."

The five months that had passed had seemed like a lifetime. If she told him she was ready now, would it be the truth? Would he believe her?

"We could start over," she suggested.

"As what? Colleagues who once had sex and now are trying to renew a friendship?"

His words hit her solar plexus squarely, just where he'd intended. Yet she couldn't give up. "Maybe," she answered truthfully. "We can't deny what happened, but I hate this...wall between us. You were there when Grace and Sophie were born, and now you've just dropped out of their lives."

"I thought the emails—"

"Mitch, you sent them from a sense of duty, because you made a promise to Troy. I didn't know if you really cared. I didn't know whether to email you pictures or describe how I rolled their strollers through the sprinkler and they loved it, or how their hair was finally long enough to put little bows in."

He dropped his hand from her shoulder as if he could see the pictures, too, the pictures of *them* as they'd been, not just the twins. "I walked away because it was the right thing to do."

"For *me* or for *you?*"

"For both of us."

He didn't look or sound as if he had any regrets. That hurt—a lot. She shook her head and accepted what seemed to be inevitable. "If you want to just be colleagues, that's fine. We'll figure out eventually how to relate on that level."

She would have gone again, but this time the huskiness in his voice stopped her. "Lily."

When she swung around suddenly, she saw a flicker of something on his face...and she waited, hoping.

"What did you have in mind?" he asked.

If that wasn't a loaded question! But she did have

something in mind. She just didn't know if he'd go for it.

"How are you celebrating Thanksgiving?" Lily asked. It was only three days away. If he had plans, so be it. She'd figure out something else.

"I plan to pick up a turkey dinner at the Yellow Rose."

She noticed the lines around Mitch's mouth seemed deeper. "And take it home and eat it alone?"

"I guess that's not how most people celebrate Thanksgiving, but afterward I was going to make some phone calls, to make sure everyone was still coming next weekend."

His reunion weekend. The one she'd thought she'd be involved in. "Would you like to come along with Ellie and me to Raina and Shep's?"

Considering that for a few heartbeats, Mitch finally answered, "Are you sure they wouldn't mind having an unexpected guest?"

Her heart seemed to jump against her chest. "Shep said Eva bought a turkey big enough to fill the entire oven. I'm sure they won't mind."

"You already checked this out with Raina, didn't you?" he asked suspiciously.

"Actually, it was her idea. I mentioned things were strained between us here."

"Women," he said with a bit of exasperation. "Do you have to tell each other *everything?*"

"Not everything," Lily assured him quickly.

There was a darkening of Mitch's eyes and she knew he'd caught her underlying meaning.

"Ellie might not like the idea," he pointed out.

"No, she might not. And for her sake, it might be better if we meet at Shep and Raina's ranch."

"Doesn't this take us back where we started?" he asked with such soberness she realized much more was going on under the surface than he was revealing.

"No, it doesn't. Because I'll tell her I invited you. I'll make that clear."

It was easy for her to see that Mitch was debating with himself.

Although she didn't want to say acceptable words just because he wanted to hear them, she did. "If you don't want to come, that's okay. I understand. I just thought maybe we could ease back into…friendship."

"With a crowd around?" he asked, the corner of his lip quirking up.

"Sometimes conversation comes more easily that way."

"And kids are always great buffers."

"Yes," she agreed, now holding her breath, waiting for his answer.

He gave it in the form of another question. "What time does Thanksgiving dinner start?"

When Raina pulled Mitch into a bedlam of bubbling voices, running kids and chattering adults, he knew he must be crazy. He could be sitting home alone, in front of a takeout turkey dinner—

His gaze found Lily right off. At the stove, she was testing the boiling potatoes. Her hair was arranged in a wispy version of a bun that made his fingers tingle to pull it down. She was wearing a calf-length suede skirt with tan boots, and a long multicolored blouse with a concho belt slung low on her slim waist. When she turned to wave at him, he could read her apron that proclaimed in block lettering, I'd Rather Cook Than Clean.

As Shep came toward him, Mitch offered him a bottle of wine. To Raina, he handed a bouquet of colorful mums.

"You didn't have to do that," she said.

"I wanted to." He really had. It was nice of them to include him.

How much did Lily want him here? Maybe she just wanted them to work together without snubbing each other. That would be a far cry from becoming friends again. Friends like before Troy had died? Or friends like after the twins were born?

Lily's babies were sitting in play saucers in the kitchen so she could keep her eye on them. Eva was conversing with Ellie as they made a salad together. Ellie had given Mitch a glance and lifted a hand in his direction, but that was about all.

This could be one interesting Thanksgiving dinner.

Although he knew it wasn't in his best interest, he did want to see how Sophie and Grace had grown.

It had been more than difficult to stay away from Lily and her daughters all these months. But he'd felt it was the right move to make. She'd needed time to recover from Troy's passing. And even now he doubted enough time had passed. But today was about getting a real look at her life again. If he had to try to watch over her without getting involved, then somehow he'd manage that.

He hunkered down at Grace's play saucer, helping her ring a bell, spin a wheel and study her face in the mirror. She giggled at him and reached out to touch his jaw. That tiny hand on his chin made his heart squeeze uncomfortably, so he gave it a gentle pat and moved on to Sophie, who seemed a little more sedate. After all, she was the older sister, even if it was only by two to three minutes. She was slower to let Mitch join in her private game, but eventually she welcomed the intricacies of his set of keys and would have kept them if not for her mom intervening.

"She'll put them in her mouth," Lily said. "I try to keep her toys as sterile as possible, but you know how that is."

"Actually, I don't, but I can imagine with their crawling all over the floor." He looked around at the saucers and stroller and the high chairs. "You must have brought a truck."

Lily laughed.

"The high chairs and stroller fold. Ellie stowed them in the back of her car." She glanced back at the potatoes. "I'd better finish those if we want them ready with the turkey."

"Do you need help with the pot?" It was huge and, he imagined, quite heavy.

"Sure. That would be great."

As he stepped around her, his hip brushed hers. That minor connection of their bodies threw him more than he wanted to admit. He stood in front of the stove and reached for the pot. As always with Lily, physical contact sent his system into a rush forward toward something out of his reach. He thought that might have diminished in their time apart.

It hadn't.

Coming here today had been stupid. He avoided her gaze as he drained the potatoes into a colander in the sink, steam billowing up all around them. *This isn't the first time,* he thought ironically.

"Into the mixing bowl?" he asked, looking at the bowl on the counter.

She nodded, avoiding his gaze, too.

They were a pair. No, *not* a pair, he corrected himself. Just two individuals with wants and needs that couldn't be fulfilled.

He saw Lily go over to her daughters and consult with Raina, who was playing with them, her own five-month-old cuddled close on her lap. Then Lily returned to the mixer.

"Raina said I could put in whatever I want, so here goes."

"Whatever you want?" he asked. "I thought they just got butter and milk."

"That's the plain version," Lily explained with a smile, starting the mixer. "I like to add a little pizzazz."

She added pizzazz all right. With fascination, he watched her add sour cream, milk, chives and a blob of butter for good measure.

"No cholesterol there," he muttered.

She jabbed him in the ribs. "It's Thanksgiving."

He liked the feel of her friendliness again. He'd missed her a lot over the past five months. In his email inquiries, he'd wanted to ask question after question—about the babies and about her. Yet he'd known he had to, in large part, leave her alone. He should have done that to begin with. Today, however, with her close by his side, within kissing distance, inhaling the familiar scent of her perfume, he saw keeping a wall up between them was either very smart...or very stupid. What would an affair do to them? Was she even open to one? Were either of them really ready to move on?

After whipping the potatoes into a delicious white frenzy, Lily stuck in a spoon, took a fingerful and poked it into her mouth. She rolled her eyes. "Just right. Try some?"

He'd watched that finger go into her mouth. He'd watched her lips pucker up. He'd watched her lick it. If there weren't so many people in the big kitchen, he'd kiss her. But there were and he didn't. Instead he put his finger on the spoon, curled potatoes onto it and popped it into his mouth.

"Just right," he agreed, his eyes locking to hers, his gut telling him they weren't finished and might never be.

Mitch barely heard the sound of scraping chairs and laughter and the clatter of silverware.

He *did* hear the doorbell ring. Soon after, the door opened and he heard a woman's voice call, "We're here."

Shep picked up the turkey on its platter and carried it to the table, explaining to Mitch, "It's Raina's mom and brother. Ryder just got off his shift."

Mitch knew Raina's brother was a cop.

Ryder and Sonya Greystone came into the kitchen and were introduced to Mitch. Sonya said to him, "I hope you're a big eater, like Shep. I made pumpkin, apple and cherry pies, and I don't want to take any home."

Shep gave her a bear hug. "You don't have to worry about that."

Mitch had never experienced anything like this Thanksgiving celebration—so many people who seemed like family and really cared about each other. Then he realized that conclusion wasn't true. When he and his buddies and families got together, it was a similar feeling. Family meant something different to everyone, and he was suddenly glad he hadn't stayed home today and eaten dinner in front of a football game.

In the next few minutes, he helped Lily transfer the potatoes from the mixing bowl to a beautiful serving dish embellished with roses and gold trim. He stared at it for a second and Lily asked, "Mitch?"

In the midst of the holiday chaos, he said in a low voice, "This dish reminds me of one my mom used when she tried to make the holidays a celebration for the two of us."

"Holidays are supposed to be about memories and traditions and loved ones, even when they're not still with us."

He'd walked into that one. When his gaze met Lily's, he expected to see sadness on her face. Instead, he saw an emotion more poignant.

She said, "If you'll put those on the table, I'll set the twins in their high chairs."

In the next few minutes, everyone was seated around the huge, rectangular table. Even Joey and Roy seemed awed by the amount of food in front of them.

In the moment of quiet, Shep said, "Let's all give thanks for being together today."

Mitch didn't know where the chain started—maybe with Shep's children—but everyone held hands and bowed their heads, remembering Thanksgivings past, grateful for the opportunity to be together like this with more than enough food for everyone to eat.

Lily had taken Mitch's hand. He intertwined his fingers with hers and she looked over at him, her eyes questioning. He didn't have the answers to those questions. They'd have to just see where today took them.

After dinner, Mitch and Shep played a board game with Roy and Joey while Eva recorded everything she could on a video camera. Every once in a while Mitch glanced over at Eva, who was sitting on the floor beside Manuel as he rode a high-tech rocking horse. The letters of the alphabet appeared on a little screen in front of him the longer he rocked back and forth. Grace and Sophie crawled around Lily and Ellie's feet, while Raina played with her daughter in one of the play saucers.

Roy shouted, "I won," and everyone cheered as he moved his marker into the winning block.

Mitch moved to the sofa while the boys ran to the playroom for another game. Aware of Grace crawling over to him, he smiled when she sat before him and raised her arms. He knew what that meant. It had been a while since he'd held one of the twins, a while since he'd felt as if he should.

A baby's needs always trumped overthinking, so he bent and lifted her up to his lap. At nine months she was a heartbreaker. He could only imagine how beautiful she'd be as a teenager, when someone would have to protect her from overeager guys who would date her.

Grace grinned up at him and snuggled into his chest as if she were just waiting for a place to enjoy a comfortable nap.

Ellie, who'd been talking to Raina's mother and Eva across the room, came to sit beside him. She patted Grace's leg. "Tired, little one?"

"The day's celebration has wiped her out," Mitch said amiably. He didn't know what Ellie thought about his being here today.

"She only had a short nap this afternoon before we came."

Mitch touched Grace's name embroidered on the front of her pale green overalls. "Did you make this?"

"Yes, I did. I finally got the website up and running last month, and I have orders."

"So you're thinking about staying in Sagebrush?"

"That depends on Lily. Mom asked her to come back to Oklahoma and raise the twins there. That way she and my dad could see them more often and give her all the help she needs."

Mitch remained silent. Finally he said, "Lily seemed happy to get back to work. She'd have to find a practice in Oklahoma City or start her own."

"That's true. But Oklahoma City is a medical center. I don't think she'd have a problem starting over there."

Grace's tiny fingers rubbed up and down against Mitch's sweater as if it were a security blanket.

"What if Lily decides to stay in Sagebrush? Will you support that decision?" Mitch asked.

"Do you think you can convince her to do that?" Ellie asked in return.

"This isn't about convincing. It's about what Lily wants and where she wants to raise her daughters."

"You sound so removed from it. Don't you care?"

Oh, he cared. More than he wanted to admit—more than he dared to admit. "I won't persuade Lily one way or the other. She has to make up her own mind. If she doesn't, she'll have regrets."

"She asked you here today." Ellie's voice was almost accusing.

"I'm not sure why she did. As you know, we haven't seen each other for a while." Ellie was the type of woman who wanted the cards on the table, so he might as well put them there.

"You two have a connection," Ellie said softly. "One anyone can see."

"Anyone can?"

"You can't hide it, even though you both try."

Mitch smoothed his hand over Grace's hair, tweaking the little green bow with his finger. "And how do you feel about that?" he asked Ellie.

"I don't think it matters how I feel."

"Yes, it does." Mitch could tell Ellie that she was the reason he and Lily hadn't been in real contact since June. On the other hand, she wasn't actually the root of the problem.

"Lily asked you here today without my input," Ellie confided.

Mitch gave Ellie a regarding look. "What would your input have been?"

Ellie kept silent.

So he said something he probably shouldn't have. "I think Lily feels she needs your permission to move on."

That widened Ellie's eyes. "You're not serious."

"Yes, I am. We probably shouldn't even be having this conversation, but I thought it would be better if we cleared the air. I don't know what's going to happen next, but I do know Lily deserves to be happy."

He'd said too much. He'd tried to take himself out of the equation as much as possible, but that was difficult when he thought he had a stake in it. It was difficult when he felt as if Lily and the twins owned a piece of his heart.

Seeing them talking, Lily crossed to the sofa with

Sophie in her arms. Sophie was rubbing her eyes and her face against Lily's blouse. "I think we'd better get these two home. In a few minutes they're either both going to be asleep or fussing because they're tired."

Mitch carefully picked up Grace and stood with her. "I'll help you pack the car. I should be going, too."

"I can take Grace," Ellie said, reaching for the little girl.

Mitch aided in the transfer, wondering just how seriously Lily might be thinking about moving to Oklahoma City.

While Ellie watched the twins, Lily and Mitch took baby paraphernalia outside to Ellie's car. The weather had turned colder. The late-November wind blew across the parking area and through the corral across the lane. Lily opened the car door while Mitch slid the high chairs inside, along with a diaper bag. At the trunk, he adjusted the stroller to lay flat.

After he shut the lid, he regarded Lily in the glow of the floodlight shining from the back of the house. "Ellie tells me Troy's mother wants you to move to Oklahoma City." He'd never intended to start like that, but the question had formed before he could think of anything else to say.

Although she wore a suede jacket, Lily wrapped her arms around herself as if to ward off a chill. "I'm surprised she told you that."

"Were *you* going to tell me?"

"I don't know. After the past few months…" She trailed off. "If I went to Oklahoma City, you wouldn't have to worry about your promise to Troy."

"Is *that* why you'd move?"

She turned away, as if making eye contact was too difficult, as if she couldn't be as honest if she did.

But he clasped her arm and pulled her a little closer. "What do you want, Lily? A different life in Oklahoma?"

"I'm thinking about it. I have good friends here, but Troy's parents are Sophie and Grace's grandparents. I'm not sure what the right thing to do is."

"Whatever makes you happy."

She gave a short laugh. "And how do we ever really know what that will be?"

He'd meant it when he'd told Ellie he wouldn't try to persuade Lily one way or the other. They'd have to set aside the question of her moving…for now. "I'm glad you asked me to come today," he said after a long pause.

"Are you?" Lily's voice was filled with the same longing Mitch felt. They'd been apart and he'd hated that. He just didn't know if they should be together.

"I never experienced a holiday quite like it," he explained. "I haven't had a place to go for holidays in a long time."

"I think Sophie and Grace remember you. They're so comfortable with you."

"And how comfortable are you with everyone watching?" He swore under his breath. "That didn't come out right."

"Yes, it did. I know what you mean. But we weren't really together today, were we?"

He had to make a decision now, which way was he going to go with Lily. He could just cut her out of his life. But wasn't that in itself making a decision for her?

"How would you like to go to the tree-lighting

ceremony on Sunday at the library? We can show the twins all the lights and let them listen to their first Christmas carols."

She only hesitated a few moments. "I'd like to do that."

He didn't ask her if she'd ever been to the tree-lighting ceremony with Troy. He didn't want to know. Although he longed to take her in his arms and kiss her, he didn't. This time, they were going to take small steps toward each other to find out if that's where they wanted to be.

Maybe Sunday would be a beginning. Maybe Sunday would be an end.

At least he'd know one way or the other.

Chapter Ten

"It pays to have connections," Mitch said with a grin as he stood inside the library, peering out the long window with Sophie in his arms. Raina's mother was the head librarian and had told them they could settle inside for as long as they wanted.

Lily was holding Grace, peering outside beside Mitch. Her arm was brushing his. Every time it did, he remembered everything about their night together—everything about her hands on his body and the shake-up of his soul. Not for the first time he wondered if he wanted Lily simply because he shouldn't have her.

Mitch suddenly felt a hand on his shoulder and tensed. As he turned, he relaxed. "Hello, Mr. Fieldcrest. Are you and your wife going to enjoy the tree-lighting ceremony?" Tucker Fieldcrest and his wife owned the

B&B where his friends would be staying this coming weekend.

"We surely are. I was going to call you this week, but now I don't have to. I just wanted to tell you, we're all ready for your guests."

Mitch introduced Tucker to Lily. They all chatted for a few minutes and then Tucker motioned to the crowd gathering outside. "They're almost ready to light the tree. You'd better get your place. I'll see you Friday night." With a wave, he left through the library's huge wooden double doors.

"He seems very nice," Lily said, after the older man had gone outside.

"He and his wife Belinda are good people. They're cutting us a break, only charging half the normal room rates. They insisted they'd be empty this time of year anyway, and our veterans deserve more than reasonable room charges."

"Absolutely," Lily said emphatically, and Mitch knew what she was thinking about. Yet she surprised him when she asked, "So, do you still need activities for the kids? Would you like me to come over and paint faces?"

"I roped Matt into playing Santa Claus and I was hoping that would take up the whole afternoon. But if you're still willing, I'm sure everyone would appreciate it."

"I'm still willing."

To do more than face paint? he wanted to ask. All the words that passed between them seemed to have an underlying message. When he'd asked her to come along tonight, he'd thought of it as a sort of date. But did she think about it that way, too? Did having the twins along make it merely an outing they could enjoy together?

He'd drive himself crazy with the questions, especially when Lily looked at him with those big, blue eyes and a smile that again brought back their night together in vivid detail. It was ironic, really. They'd had sex in the dark but every moment of it was emblazoned in his mind in living color. Sometimes he thought he could see those same pictures running through Lily's thoughts, but that could be wishful thinking.

"Let's get Sophie and Grace bundled up so we don't miss their expressions when the tree lights glow. Do you have your camera?"

Lily patted the pocket of her yellow down jacket. "Right here. But I don't know how we're going to hold them both and take their picture at the same time."

"We'll figure out something," he assured her. Sophie suddenly took hold of his nose and squeezed it a little, babbling new consonant sounds as she did. He laughed. "Getting impatient, are you? Come on, let's cover that pretty blond hair with your hat and hood so you stay warm."

Once the girls were dressed, Mitch and Lily pushed the stroller down the side ramp to the sidewalk. A fir tree stood on the land in front of the eighty-year-old, two-story brick library. The storefronts farther up the street were all lit up with multicolor lights, more than ready for Christmas shoppers. Grady Fitzgerald owned a saddle shop in the next block and Mitch thought he caught a glimpse of him and Francesca with their little boy on the other side of the tree. Lily waved to Tessa and Vince Rossi, who'd brought their children, Sean and Natalie, to watch the ceremony.

"Gina and Logan are here somewhere," Lily said to Mitch, leaning close to him so he could hear her amidst the buzz of people talking.

She pulled the camera from her pocket. "You hold the stroller and I'll take your picture."

"Lily, I don't think—" But before he could protest, before he could say he hated to have his picture taken, she'd already done it. Turnabout was fair play, so he motioned her to the back of the stroller, snagged the camera from her hand and took more than one of her with her girls. Sophie and Grace seemed to be mesmerized by the people passing by, the stand with the microphone where the mayor stood, the wind carrying the smells of French fries, corn dogs and hamburgers from the food cart parked not far away.

As the mayor, Greta Landon, came to the mike and started her remarks, Mitch handed the camera back to Lily. He swooped Sophie out of the stroller and said, "If you hand me Grace, I can hold them both up, and you can take their picture when the lights go on."

After Lily lifted Grace from the stroller, she transferred her to Mitch. As she stood close, she tilted her chin up and was almost near enough to kiss. She said, "This was a great idea. Maybe we'll start a tradition."

If you don't leave Sagebrush for Oklahoma City, he thought. He believed he was so good at not giving anything away, but he must have been wrong about that. Because Lily backed away as if she couldn't reassure him she would be staying in Texas. Her impulsive exclamation had been just that—impulsive.

Just like their night together.

At that moment, the mayor announced, "Let this

year's Christmas tree glow brightly for all the residents of Sagebrush."

The tree came alive with blue, red, green and purple balls. Strand after strand of tiny white lights twinkled around those. Mitch witnessed the expression on Sophie and Grace's faces, and their wide-eyed awe was priceless.

Instead of looking at the tree when the Christmas carols began playing, Lily's face was Madonna-like as she gazed at her girls. Then her eyes locked to his. Something elemental twisted in his chest.

The twins already seemed to be developing their own language. They babbled to each other and the gibberish was almost in a cadence that Mitch thought of as language.

Lily leaned in and kissed both of their cheeks, then snapped a picture of Mitch holding them. "What do you think of all those lights?"

They waved their hands at each other and at her.

All of a sudden, Hillary was at Lily's side, carrying her own daughter. "Look who's here," Hillary said, taking in Mitch, Lily and the twins. "Since when are you two seeing each other outside of the office?"

"Since tonight," Mitch answered, matter-of-factly. "We're sharing some Christmas cheer. How does Megan like all this?" If there was one thing Mitch knew, it was that talking about someone's children always took their mind off anything else.

Still, Hillary gave him a knowing look. "She loved it, but now I think she's ready for bed. Besides, I don't want her out in the cold too long. How about you? Are you going to go back into the library for some complimentary hot chocolate?"

He and Lily hadn't discussed that, but he imagined what her answer would be. "We're headed home, too."

Hillary shifted Megan to her other arm. "Well, it was good to run into you without your lab coats on. I'll see you tomorrow." Then as quickly as she'd appeared, she was gone.

If Lily was going to take issue with what he'd told Hillary, this wasn't the time or place. He said, "Let's get them into the stroller and roll them to the car, unless you really would like some hot chocolate first."

As Lily took Sophie from him, she replied, "We can make hot chocolate back at the house."

Hmm. They just might be in for that discussion after all.

Lily had been surprised tonight at what Mitch had said to Hillary. For all those months he'd seemed as far away as the North Pole. But when he'd asked her to come along with him tonight, he seemed to have established a now-or-never attitude. However, everything was unsaid. Everything was up in the air. Everything was up to them.

How should she feel about his proprietary statement? Were they going to be a couple? Could Mitch make a lifelong commitment if that's where they were headed? What if she decided she shouldn't stay in Sagebrush? All the questions were terrifying, along with the life changes they could provoke.

But for tonight?

The warm and fuzzy feelings from the tree-lighting ceremony lingered as they drove home.

After they pulled into the drive, gathered the girls and the stroller and rolled them up the front walk, Mitch asked, "How will your housemates feel about us coming back here?"

"I guess we'll find out."

Her flippant reply almost seemed like a challenge.

Once in the living room, he found Angie and Ellie watching a forensic drama on TV while they strung popcorn to use as garlands.

"You're getting ready for Christmas?" he asked as a hello.

Ellie looked up, shot him a forced smile, then went back to stringing.

Angie responded to his question. "We all like to do home-crafted decorations, so it can take a while."

Without thinking twice, he took Sophie from her stroller, unzipped her coat, took off her mittens and hat and picked her up.

"Ma-ma-ma-ma," she said practically, as her sister chimed in with the same syllable.

He laughed and asked Lily, "Two bottles upstairs?"

She nodded.

"If you need some help..." Ellie called.

"You look like you're busy," Mitch said. "We'll be okay." Taking the lead was second nature to him. Would Lily mind? She didn't give any indication that she did.

"I put bottles together," Angie said. "They're in the refrigerator in their bedroom."

Mitch glanced over his shoulder as he carried Sophie upstairs, right behind Lily with Grace. He wasn't surprised to see Ellie's gaze on them.

In the twins' bedroom, Mitch and Lily stole glances at each other while they fed the girls and readied them for bed. They'd been super-aware of each other all night, but hadn't been able to act on that awareness. Now they still couldn't, with Sophie and Grace to care for and Ellie and Angie downstairs. The whole situation was frustrating, titillating and exciting. Mitch knew he'd thrown down a figurative gauntlet tonight, and Lily had to make the decision whether or not she wanted to pick it up. She could deny their bond as she had once before. Maybe he was just waiting for her to do it again. Maybe he wanted the safer route. Maybe living alone was preferable to caring about a family. Maybe he didn't think he deserved a family. Because he had come home but others hadn't?

It was a lonely route, yet he was used to it.

Once the twins were comfortably settled in their cribs, once Lily had kissed them both and he'd simply laid a protective hand on each of their foreheads, Lily and Mitch left them to sleep by the glow of the night-light and stepped into the hall. This was about the most privacy they were going to have.

At least that's what he thought until Lily said, "I need to turn on their monitor in my bedroom."

Lily's bedroom. Visions raced through his mind.

Lily went ahead to her nightstand and switched on the monitor. He stepped over the threshold and shut the door.

She didn't move and neither did he for a moment. Then he saw that flicker in her eyes, the memory of what it was like when they were together. He covered the two steps to her, lifted her chin and looked deep into her eyes. "I told Hillary we were dating."

"I know."

"Do you have an opinion about that?"

"I didn't protest."

"No, mainly so you wouldn't embarrass us both."

"That wasn't the reason."

"What was?" he demanded, tired of waiting, yet knowing that with Lily all he could do was wait until she was truly free of yesterday.

"Because I want to spend time with you, Mitch— *with* the twins...*without* the twins. I can't tell you everything's going to go smoothly. I still miss Troy." She looked down at her hand, and he did, too. Her wedding ring glistened there, as real now as the day Troy had slipped it on her finger.

"And *I'm* used to being alone," he admitted.

"Do you like that?" she asked with the spirit that was all Lily.

He almost laughed. Almost. But the question had been a serious one. "I used to think being alone was the only way I could deal with my life on my terms."

"And now?"

"I'm open to finding out differently. That's all I can give you right now."

The expression on her pretty face said she didn't know if that was enough. He didn't, either. But as he bent his head, kissing her seemed a lot more important than the future.

He brushed his lips against hers, maybe to test her, to see how much she wanted. But the test became his to pass or fail. She responded by twining her arms around his neck and slipping her fingers into his hair. He'd wanted to take everything slowly with Lily. This time they'd take it easy. This time he'd make sure she knew what she was doing. This time, she wouldn't want to deny what was going on between them.

But the moment her fingers tugged at his hair as if

she wanted more, undeniable desire rushed through his body.

Making himself slow down, he kissed her neck, and asked, "How much time do you think we have?" He leaned back to check her expression, to see if she felt guilty about being in her room with him, to see if what her housemates thought mattered.

"A few minutes," she responded. "Ellie and Angie will wonder if everything's all right."

A few minutes wasn't enough time. So he didn't waste a moment more of it. His mouth came down on hers possessively, coaxing, teasing, plundering. Still the moan that came from Lily's throat gave the kiss more power as they both gave in to the primal quality of it. He thrust his tongue into her mouth, felt her soft, full breasts against him, and knew he was more aroused than he'd ever been. His hands slid down her back and he pressed her into him. She shivered and the trembling of her body made him wonder what he was doing. Their kisses awakened him to the raw need inside him. What if that need could never be satisfied? What if Lily, too, turned away from his scars? After all, the last time, they'd made love in the dark. What if he had a nightmare while he was lying beside her? How would she react?

The questions flooding his brain doused the far-reaching, fiery tendrils of his desire. A good thing, too, because he might have pulled her onto that bed, undressed her and joined their bodies no matter who was downstairs.

Tearing himself from her and the kiss, he stood away so he wouldn't reach for her again.

Looking a bit dazed, she said, "Wow! Those few minutes sure went fast."

He rubbed his hand over his face. "You get to me."

Smiling, she replied, *"You* get to *me."*

What bothered Mitch was that, despite the rush of passion that had enfolded them, the smile on Lily's face and in her voice didn't touch her eyes. Neither of them seemed happy about it.

"I'm looking forward to this weekend, Lily, but if you don't want to take the time away from Sophie and Grace, I'll understand. I'll be busy playing host, so I don't know how much time I'll have for...us."

Her hands fluttered as if she didn't know what to do with them, so she stuffed them into her front jeans pockets. "Why don't we just play it by ear? I'll see what kind of day the girls are having and then decide."

"Fair enough," he responded. Yet what he'd suggested didn't seem fair at all. He'd just given her an out, and she might take it...just as she might still move to Oklahoma City and leave her life in Sagebrush behind.

Midweek, Lily softly descended the steps into the living room, not wanting to awaken anyone. Sophie and Grace were snuggled in for the night. Angie, on day shift now, had turned in around the same time as Ellie after the evening news.

But Lily couldn't sleep. The decision whether or not to go to Mitch's on Saturday was gnawing at her. Every time she ran into him during the course of the day, she knew he was wondering if she'd be there or not. She felt that if she decided to go, she would be making a commitment.

A commitment to Mitch when she still wore her wedding ring?

She'd had lunch with Raina today, who had given her

a DVD copy of the video Eva had recorded on Thanksgiving. Lying in bed, feeling more alone than she'd ever remembered feeling, Lily decided she needed to watch that DVD.

After she inserted the disk in the machine, she sat on the sofa, perched on the edge of the cushion, pressing the buttons on the remote. The video sprang to life and she watched Thanksgiving Day come alive for her all over again. The living room at Shep and Raina's had been full of lively chatter. Mitch sat on the floor with Joey and Roy, his long legs stretched out in front of him, crossed at the ankles. The boys said something and Mitch laughed. He had such a deep, rich laugh and she rarely heard it. But he'd laughed often on Thanksgiving Day. Because he'd been relaxed? Because kids surrounded him? Because the two of them were together with friends in a way they hadn't been before?

The moment Grace raised her arms to Mitch and he'd lifted her onto his lap brought tears to Lily's eyes. He was so caring and gentle with the girls. Yet Lily sensed he still withheld part of himself. He didn't want to get too attached. Because in being attached to them, he'd be attached to her?

"You should be asleep," a soft voice scolded.

Startled, Lily dropped the remote.

"Sorry," Ellie said, coming to sit beside her. "I didn't mean to scare you."

Bending to the floor, Lily found the remote and hit the stop button.

"This is Thanksgiving," Ellie noticed, staring at the freeze frame on the TV, the still image of Mitch holding Grace.

"Raina gave me a copy today. She thought I'd like to

have it for posterity," Lily said with a small, short laugh that she had to force out.

"You don't have to stop it on my account. I was there, remember?"

"I know, but I thought—"

"Stop tiptoeing around me, Lily. You don't have to. I know how I reacted at the beginning of the summer when Mitch was around. I'm sorry for that."

"You had every right to feel whatever you were feeling."

"I had no right to dictate who you should or shouldn't see."

"You didn't."

"Then why didn't I see Mitch around for almost six months?"

"That was *my* fault, not yours. I wasn't ready to open my heart to another man."

Ellie pointed to the screen. "It looks as if you're trying to figure out if you're ready now."

"If I have to figure it out, that means I'm not?" Lily asked, in turmoil about it. Yet that's what she was feeling.

"I don't know, Lily. Troy is still real to me. He's still my brother. I talk to him, and I listen for his advice. Is that crazy or what?"

"I don't think that's crazy at all. I still do that, too."

"Then maybe you should ask him about this," Ellie advised her.

The two women sat there for a few moments in the dark, with the silence, staring at the frozen picture on the TV in all its color and high definition.

Now that she and Ellie were having an open talk about this, Lily went to her purse on the foyer table and removed her camera. It had been in there since Sunday night.

"I want to show you something," she said to Ellie, sitting beside her sister-in-law again.

She switched on the camera, pressed the review button and brought up a picture. She was standing in front of the town's Christmas tree with the twins in their stroller. Then there were a few shots of Sophie and Grace by themselves, their faces filled with awe, the excitement of their first Christmas shining from their eyes. The miracle of Christmas was starting to unfold for them. She wanted the holiday to be filled with kindness and love and sharing so they'd never forget the importance of giving all year.

The final picture was Mitch holding Sophie and Grace, gazing into the camera with the intensity that was all his. Even though he was smiling, she knew he had questions about what the future held for all of them. Their attraction to each other couldn't be denied. But it muddied the already stirred-up waters. As Lily studied his face, her heart tripped. Her gaze fell to his smile and her stomach somersaulted. Staring at him holding her twins, she felt as if she could melt.

Lily flipped again to the photo of herself with Sophie and Grace, then the other one with Mitch. She said in almost a whisper, "I'm falling in love with him, and it terrifies me."

"Why?"

"Because I've lost everyone who loves me. Because Mitch has an area of his life he won't open to me. Because I'm still attached to Troy and afraid to let go."

"So what are you trying to decide?"

"Mitch's reunion with his buddies from Iraq is this

weekend. Saturday they'll be at his place most of the day and he asked me to come over. I'll be setting foot in an area of his life he kept closed off to me. He said we won't have much time alone, but after everyone leaves, we might."

"Are you asking my permission?" Ellie asked with a hint of a smile.

"No. I guess what I'm asking for is your blessing."

Ellie's gaze dropped to the end table by the sofa where a picture of Lily and Troy stood. Then she lifted it to the TV screen. "Go, Lily. You have to. It's the only way you'll know for sure if you're ready to move on. That's the best I can do."

Lily switched off the DVD player and set the camera on the coffee table. "Let's have a cup of hot cider. I want your opinion on what I'm thinking of giving to Angie and Raina for Christmas."

"You want to be distracted from what's really going on in your mind."

Ellie knew her too well because she was right.

Chapter Eleven

Mitch opened his door to Lily, trying to adjust his thinking about today to include her in it. His gut always twisted a little when he saw her...when her blue eyes looked at him with so many questions he wasn't sure he'd ever be able to answer. "I wasn't sure you'd come."

She had a cake holder in one hand, a paint case in the other. "I told you yesterday that I'd come to help."

Yes, she had. They'd been passing in the hall and she'd stopped him with a touch of her hand on his elbow. He'd felt the heat from it the rest of the day, though he'd told himself that was impossible. Had his caresses branded her the same way?

Stepping aside so she could enter, not sure what her presence meant, he pointed to the far end of the kitchen.

"I put the desserts on the table. The deli trays are in the fridge and the barbecued beef is in the slow cooker."

"It sounds as if you have all of the bases covered."

Except the base with her on it. He nodded to her carrying case. "Paints?" The mundane conversation had to get them through, although the question he wanted to ask was—would she stay the night? Too much to expect?

"Yep. And I have some board games and puzzles in the car. Along with Santa Claus, you should have the kids covered."

"I have a table set up for you in the sunroom."

After she unzipped her parka, he moved behind her, taking it from her shoulders. He hadn't been *this* close to Lily all week, though each time he'd passed her in the hall he'd wanted to haul her over his shoulder, carry her to a closet for privacy and kiss her. She'd left her hair loose today and he caught the scent of it as his hands closed over her jacket and red scarf. She was wearing a Christmas-red sweater with black jeans, dangling gold earrings and black shoe-boots with tall heels. She looked incredible.

When she glanced over her shoulder, their gazes collided and he bent his head to kiss her.

But that kiss wasn't to be. His doorbell rang and he swore under his breath. Not that he didn't want to see his visitors. But every private moment with Lily was precious.

"I'm nervous," she admitted with a shaky smile, as he hung her jacket and scarf over his arm.

"Why?"

"Because these are your friends and I'm not sure I belong here."

"I felt that way at Thanksgiving until Raina and Shep made me feel comfortable. Relax, Lily. These are just families who share a common bond. *You* share it, too."

His words didn't seem to reassure her. He wanted to wipe the anxious look off her face with a touch...with a few kisses. But he couldn't. His guests were arriving and he had to play host.

The next half hour passed in a whirlwind of guests entering and introductions being made. Lily had no trouble making conversation, as Mitch had known she wouldn't. She was easily drawn to the moms with kids, and to one of Mitch's best friends, Matt Gates, who was an ER doctor in Houston. After everyone else had arrived, Jimmy Newcomb's wife, Robin, drove their van into a space the guests had left for them in Mitch's driveway. All of the guys went outside in case Robin needed help. But the Newcomb's van was equipped with a wheelchair lift and, fortunately, Mitch's house had only one step to navigate to push the wheelchair inside.

"I don't want to make tracks in your carpet," Jimmy said to Mitch as he wheeled into the kitchen.

"You can go anywhere you want to in my house," Mitch assured him.

Robin and Maya, Tony Russo's wife, set up the kids in the sunroom with games and puzzles, drawing paper, pencils and crayons, while Lily arranged her face paints on a small table. The children began asking questions right away and she explained what she could do. Soon they were lined up, pleading with her to paint a Christmas tree or an angel, a reindeer or a butterfly on their faces. Once when Mitch looked in on her she was telling them about Christmas traditions around the world.

Another time, the children were explaining how they celebrated Christmas. He realized how much he wanted Lily to stay tonight. It had to be *her* decision. As she took a few breaks, he suspected she was calling Ellie to check on Sophie and Grace.

In the course of the afternoon, he attempted to spend time with everyone. He lit a fire in the fireplace, pulled bottles of beer from a cooler, made pots of coffee. When darkness fell, he set out the food. He'd ordered more than enough, and he was glad to see all his guests looked pleased to be there, sitting near the predecorated Christmas tree he'd bought at the last minute. Reunions could bomb. But this group had too much in common. Feelings ran deep and so did loyalties.

Matt had brought his Santa paraphernalia and stowed it in a spare bedroom where Mitch had stacked presents for the kids.

As most of the guests enjoyed dessert and Lily sat on the couch deep in conversation with Robin, Matt beckoned Mitch to follow him into the hall.

"Ready to sweat in that Santa suit?" Mitch asked with a grin.

Matt grimaced. "You're going to owe me for this one."

"Not if I can help it. You're going to love doing this so much you'll want to do it every year. If the gifts are too heavy in that flannel sack—"

"Do you think practicing in the ER is making me soft?" Matt inquired with a raised brow.

"Not for a minute," Mitch assured him.

"Before I forget, I want to give you something," Matt said, taking out his wallet and slipping out a business card.

"What's this?" Mitch glanced at it and saw the name, address and telephone number of a doctor—the head of the Hand and Trauma Surgery division at the hospital where Matt practiced.

"Eric Dolman is good, Mitch. The best I've ever seen. He's performed nerve grafting and conduits, as well as nerve transfers, with success. If you want to return to surgery, you might want to fly to Houston to see him. I could probably get you in on short notice."

Mitch's gut tightened. "I have a new career now. I was told surgery could cause more damage than I already have." He flexed his fingers just thinking about it.

"Look, Mitch. I know about survivor guilt. Most of us carry it. Maybe it's time to lose it and reach out for something you deserve to have. If you don't want to go back to trauma surgery, that's your decision. But Eric might be able to restore full use of your hand."

Mitch heard a noise and swung around. Lily was standing there and had obviously cleared her throat to make her presence known. She was holding her cell phone and probably looking for a quiet place to make her call.

"I didn't mean to interrupt," she told both of them. "I was just trying to find—"

"A little quiet?" Matt filled in with a smile. "That's hard to do around this crowd." His grin faded, then he became serious. "Tony's wife told me you lost your husband to Afghanistan. I'm sorry."

"Thank you," Lily replied, looking down at her phone where a picture of her twins stared up at her.

Matt tapped the card Mitch was still holding. "Don't lose that. Call him anytime. Just mention my name." Then he strode down the hall to the bedroom.

Lily's blue eyes found Mitch's. "I really didn't mean to interrupt. I overheard a little. This doctor could repair the damage to your hand?"

If Mitch was going to even think about doing this, he had to run it through his own mind first. "The risk could be greater than the rewards."

"But if you could return to surgery—"

"Lily, I don't think this is the time or place to have this discussion. Can we just table it for now?"

"Does that mean you'll want to talk about it later?" she challenged.

Not only was Mitch hesitating to start a serious relationship with Lily because of her memories...but also because of his. She might want too much from him, a closeness he didn't know how to give. She was pushing him now, and that made him restless and uncomfortable. So he was honest with her. "I don't know. I need some time to think about what Matt said. I might want to research this doctor. I might not want to discuss surgery at all."

He saw the hurt on Lily's face, and he knew he was closing her out. But this was sacred territory to him. She didn't understand the ramifications of everything surgery could stir up. Not only memories of his time in the hospital and rehab, working to change his specialty to endocrinology, but also the cause of it all. He didn't talk about *that* to anyone.

More gently, he told her, "I'm going to set up the kindling in the fire pit. After Santa leaves, we can toast marshmallows with the kids."

"I'm sure they'll like that," Lily said, much too politely.

He left her in the hall, believing that after the marshmallows were toasted, she would leave.

Lily opened one side of the French doors and stepped outside onto the red-and-gray brick patio. It was huge, running along most of the back of Mitch's house. But three high stone walls framed the outside of the patio, giving it a protective feel. Mitch, Jimmy and Matt sat by the fire, talking, mugs of hot coffee in their hands.

She walked over to them, zipping her parka. "The kids want to come out and sing Christmas carols before they all go back to the bed-and-breakfast."

"Tell them to come on," Mitch said, rising to his feet.

Lawn chairs were scattered across the bricks, where after Santa's arrival and departure some of the older children had toasted marshmallows for the younger ones under their parents' watchful eyes. Now the fire had died down and short flames licked at the remaining logs under the mesh fire screen.

Lily didn't have to convey Mitch's invitation to the guests inside. As soon as she turned toward the door again, all the children and adults who had gone for their coats poured out. Light from inside shone on the closest section of the patio. The rest was lit by a half moon and so many stars she couldn't count them all if she tried. For Mitch's guests who lived in cities, this had to be a treat. Those who lived in more rural areas knew how to appreciate the beauty of the winter night.

Jimmy's little boy, who was eight and had Rudolph painted on one cheek, grabbed Lily's hand and pulled her toward his mom and dad. "Stand over here," he told her.

She did and found herself beside Mitch.

The night was turning colder and a light wind blew over the stone walls, but she felt protected in the cocoon of the patio, although her breath puffed white vapor in front of her.

Beside her husband, Robin suggested, "Let's take hands."

A hush fell over the group and even the little ones reached for a hand on either side of them. Lily found one of her hands in Mitch's, the other holding Jimmy's. She was emotionally moved in a way she couldn't even begin to express, especially when Maya's sweet voice began "Silent Night." Lily's throat closed as she tried to sing along with the words.

All is calm. All is bright.

How these men deserved calmness and bright.

Instead of holding her hand now, Mitch swung his arm around her shoulders.

What was he feeling at this moment? What had this night meant to him? Would he talk to her about it? Would he talk to her about the possible surgery?

Sleep in heavenly peace. Sleep in heavenly peace.

She suspected all the men were thinking about fallen comrades and maybe how lucky and grateful they were to be alive…to be here together. She thought about the Purple Heart medal tucked away in her jewelry box and how well Troy would have fit in here tonight.

After the last verse of the Christmas carol, moms and dads herded up children and one by one thanked Mitch for his hospitality. She heard him say, "It'll be your turn sometime. Then I'll be thanking you."

He'd gone to a lot of trouble to put this weekend together and it showed.

Inside the house again once more, Mitch saw his guests to the door. Lily stowed food away while he made sure Jimmy accessed his van without difficulty.

"You don't have to do that," Mitch told Lily when he returned to the kitchen.

Actually she'd been grateful for something to do. She knew what *she* wanted to happen next, but she wasn't sure how Mitch felt. "There's not much left. A few pieces of chocolate cake, a half dozen cookies. Some guacamole and a bag of corn chips."

She covered the remainder of the cake with plastic wrap and set it on the counter. "Matt was a great Santa."

"He's always the life of the party," Mitch replied.

The echo of "Silent Night" and the picture of the group gathered outside would be lasting. "Jimmy's a remarkable man. Robin explained a little of what their life is like since he became paralyzed. They're both courageous people."

"She stuck by him when he wasn't sure she would."

"She loves him."

"Sometimes love isn't enough."

Mitch's decisive words seemed to echo in the kitchen. Lily didn't know if he was going to ask her to stay the night, but if he wasn't, she wanted to discuss the surgery on his hand.

He was standing by the counter perfectly still as she moved closer to him. "Nothing can change what happened to Jimmy in Iraq." She took Mitch's hand and ran her thumb over the top of it. "But maybe you can change some of what happened to you."

Mitch pulled away from her, his expression closed. "I told you—surgery could have repercussions."

"I understand that. But a consultation would do no harm."

"I'd have to take time off."

"The practice slows down over the holidays," she reminded him.

His jaw became more set. "I don't want to be a guinea pig. I don't want to be given false hope or become a statistic."

"You haven't even *met* this doctor. You don't have the information you need to make an informed decision."

He blew out a frustrated breath. "Lily, I don't want to argue about this."

"Fine," she said agreeably. "We don't have to argue. I'm merely making a few observations." Then stepping even closer to him, laying her hand gently on his tight jaw, she whispered, "I care about you."

The tension in his body was obvious in his granite-like expression, the squareness of his shoulders, his legs defensively widened. Did it come from more than this interchange between them? After all, although he'd never admit it, this had to have been an emotional day for him.

Looking deeply into her eyes, he seemed to try to see to her very essence. She stood silent, holding her breath.

Then he covered her hand with his. They stood that way for what seemed like hours. The ice maker in the freezer rumbled as it made new ice. The heating system pinged as it battled against the cold night. Lily could feel the pulse in Mitch's jaw jumping under her palm.

Finally he dropped his hand and wrapped his arms around her. When he kissed her, his raw hunger excited her need, ratcheted up the desire that had been building between them, told them both that coming together again would be an explosion of passion.

After Mitch broke the kiss, he leaned away slightly and asked, "Will you stay tonight?"

"I thought you'd never ask," she replied a bit shakily.

Moments later, sitting on the corner of the bed in Mitch's room, her earrings in her palm, Lily ended her call with Ellie. She'd switched on one of the dresser lamps when she'd entered. Now as she glanced around, she saw Mitch's minimalist taste reflected here, too. The bed's headboard was dark pecan, as were the dresser, chest and nightstands. The lamps were a combination of wood and black iron, with the dresser top uncluttered. Yet the multicolored rug beside the bed looked handwoven. The afghan on top of the brown suede-like spread seemed to be hand-knitted.

Rising to her feet, she walked to the dresser and laid her phone and earrings there. She hadn't packed an overnight bag. Because she hadn't wanted to think tonight was a sure thing?

When Mitch entered the room, her body knew it. She didn't turn around but rather raised her gaze in the mirror.

He came up behind her, his eyes on hers. "Everything's okay at home?"

She nodded.

Sliding his arms around her, he pulled her tight against him. "We both smell like wood smoke," he growled against her ear.

Feeling him strong and hard against her body, excitement coursed through her. Her breaths became more shallow, and already she was tingling in the places she imagined he might touch.

"Wood smoke can be sexy," she teased lightly.

"*You're* sexy," he returned, his hands covering her breasts.

Lily trembled from head to toe. At that moment her need for Mitch was go great, she felt she could melt in his hands. Even though she'd stopped breast-feeding, her breasts had remained larger than they once were. Now as they lay cupped in Mitch's palms, she was grateful for every sensation, every nuance of feeling. Yet she understood that feeling would be so much greater with her clothes *off.*

"Undress me," she requested with an urgency that Mitch could obviously hear.

His low chuckle vibrated against her back. "Sometimes making out can be more scintillating with your clothes on." His hands moved down her stomach to the waistband of her jeans.

"Aren't we going to do more than make out?" she asked.

His answer was rough against her ear. "Eventually."

Mitch's foreplay was driving her crazy. All she wanted to do was crawl into bed with him, their bodies naked and exposed to each other's hands and mouths.

Before she realized what Mitch was going to do, her jeans were around her hips, held up by his thighs. His hands slid inside her panties and cupped her. She'd never felt like this—on the verge of an orgasm without even a kiss.

"Do you know how often our first time together

plays in my mind?" he asked with an erotic rasp to his words.

She had those same pictures in her mind. The continuous loop the visions made came to her at odd times and could make her blush.

His finger slipped inside of her and she moaned, needing to turn and face him.

But he wouldn't let her. "Watch in the mirror," he commanded.

There was something so sensual about what they were doing, and the way they were doing it. She'd never watched herself enjoy pleasure. When she lifted her gaze to his and stared at their reflection, his fingers started moving again. Her breath caught. She stared into his eyes as her body tensed and then released in swirls of muscle-melting sensations.

After the orgasmic release, she lay her head back against his shoulder. He held her tightly.

After a few moments of letting her catch her breath, he said, "Let's take off those boots. They make your legs look like a million bucks, but I think they could be dangerous in bed."

They undressed each other beside the bed, and this time—unlike the first—they did it by the glow of the lamp. If Mitch had given her pleasure to blunt the experience of what she was about to see, it hadn't worked. All of her senses seemed even more sensitive to everything that was revealed. His body was hard and muscled and strong, attesting to his workouts. Silky black chest hair formed a Y, arrowing down his flat stomach, around his navel. But red scars from surgery streaked his side. The heel of her hand slid over them as she sifted her fingers through his chest hair.

"Lily," he breathed, "we can just get in bed—"

"No."

She wanted to see. She wanted to know. She needed to feel.

His shoulder and arm were mottled with zigzagging scars, bumps and ridges, and she could only imagine the pain of his injury. She kissed the arm that he kept covered the whole way down to his wrist. Then she took his hand in hers and brought it to her lips.

He again murmured, "Lily—"

He'd undressed her first, but now she finished undressing him. When he kicked his jeans and briefs aside, she rested her hands on his hips and gazed up into his eyes.

Then he was kissing her and his tongue was in her mouth and hers was in his. She couldn't seem to reach far enough to explore or hold him tight enough against her to hear the beat of his heart. She wasn't even sure how they managed moving, but they fell or rolled onto the bed, so hungry for each other they didn't have enough words or touches to express it. Mitch's fingertips stroked her face. Her hand passed down his thigh and cupped his arousal. They were frantic to kiss each other all over, to explore erogenous zones, to stoke their desire to the limit. Mitch's scent had become familiar to her and now it was like an aphrodisiac she couldn't get enough of. The intensity of their foreplay made her body glisten, her heart race, her limbs quiver in anticipation of release. She didn't want to admit how, at that moment, Mitch blotted out everything else in her world. She didn't want to admit to having this mindless passion she'd never felt before. Yet she had to face what was happening, how deeply she was falling, how inexorable their attraction was.

"I need you," she confessed with sudden tears closing her throat.

Mitch reached for a condom, prepared himself, then rose above her. He took her hands, one on either side of her head, and interlocked his fingers with hers. When she raised her knees, he entered her with a thrust of possession that made her gasp. Her climax began building from the first stroke. She wrapped her legs around him, swimming in pleasure that was bigger than the ocean, wider than the universe, higher than heaven.

"Open your eyes and look at me," Mitch commanded, and she knew why. He wanted her to make sure she knew who he was.

"Mitch," she cried, assuring him she did.

His rhythm became faster. She took him deeper. The explosion that rocked them both should have blown the roof off the house.

But it didn't. It simply left them both breathless and gasping and exhausted from a union that had been months in the making.

Lily lowered her legs, loving the feel of Mitch's body on hers. She wanted to postpone the "where do we go from here" moment for as long as she could.

At first, Lily didn't know what had awakened her. A shout. Groans.

Mitch wasn't in bed with her.

Another shout and she finally was alert enough to know what was happening.

She grabbed Mitch's flannel shirt from a chair and slipped it on as she ran from his bedroom to the guest bedroom next door. Mitch was thrashing in the bed, calling a name—Larry. He was drenched in sweat, breathing hard, eyes open but unseeing.

Lily had learned about post-traumatic stress disorder but didn't know whether to awaken him, or whether to get too close. She'd read about the cut with reality that occurred when flashbacks became more real than life itself. What had triggered this? Being with fellow servicemen who knew what war was about? Sitting around the fire? Talking about surface life yet never going too deep?

Grabbing the metal waste can, she banged it against a tall, wrought-iron floor lamp. The noise was loud and seemed to penetrate Mitch's nightmare. He sat up, eyes open with awareness now, and stared at her still holding the waste can.

When he passed his hands down his face, rubbed his eyes and forehead as if to try to erase everything he'd just seen, she slid into the bed beside him and attempted to fold her arms around him.

He prevented her from doing that and pushed away.

"Everything's fine now, Mitch. I'm here."

"Your being here doesn't change what happened over there." His voice was gravelly with regret, sadness and too many memories.

"Maybe it's time you tell me about it."

"You don't want to hear this, Lily."

When she clasped his shoulder, he flinched, but she didn't remove her hand. "I might not want to hear it, but you need to say it out loud. You need to talk to somebody about it, and right now I think I'm the best person. Just stop fighting your subconscious, Mitch, and let it out."

"Do you think talking about it is going to take away the nightmares? Get *real*, Lily."

"I don't know if talking about your experience will take away anything. I suppose it could make memories worse for a while. But suffering in silence isn't the answer, either."

In that silence Lily could hear Mitch's breathing, still not quite as regular as usual. She could feel his doubt, as if revealing *anything* could make his nightmares worse. But she sat there steadfastly, her hand on his shoulder.

His voice was detached when he said, "I got used to the scud alerts, the bunkers, the MREs. It's amazing what can become normal. I not only cared for our soldiers, but for Iraqis too, many of them children with shrapnel injuries. The sound of artillery shots and mortars coming back at us became a backdrop."

Stopping, he seemed to prepare himself for remembering. Sending her a look that said he didn't want to do this and he was going to get it over with quickly, he continued, "We had spent a couple of days cross-training with ambulance teams, going over procedures. We slept when we could catch minutes, sometimes an hour."

After a quiet so prolonged she didn't know if he'd continue, he did. The nerve in his jaw worked and she could hear the strain in his voice when he said, "I was traveling in a convoy when RPGs came at us. The next thing I knew we'd hit an IED."

Lily was familiar with the military speaking in acronyms. RPG stood for rocket propelled grenade...IED, improvised explosive device.

Mitch's face took on a gray pallor as he forced himself to go on. "Blood was *everywhere*." His voice lowered. "The man beside me was...gone. At that point I didn't realize the extent of my injuries, because adrenaline raced so fast I didn't think about anything except helping anybody who was hurt. My ears rang, though. And rounds were still bouncing off the Humvee even though it was burning. I helped two men from the vehicle, but I saw others who'd been tossed out by the explosion. There was fire all around. I spotted Larry and somehow reached him. He had a hole in his thigh—the femoral vein—" Mitch closed his eyes. "Tony covered me with an M16. All I could think of was that I had to stop the bleeding. I *had* to stop it. What seemed like wild shots zinged over my head. Everything was on fire," he said again. "So I threw my body over his. I heard a muffled yell. I finally saw part of the Humvee had been blown away from the fire. I dragged Larry behind it. Someone handed me a piece of a shirt. I tried to staunch the blood. Then I…must have blacked out."

Mitch took a deep breath…stared away from her… into the past. "I had recollections of the medevac, but other than that, the next thing I knew I was waking up in a hospital in Germany, my spleen gone, internal injuries repaired, a pin in my shoulder and another in my leg."

By the time Mitch finished, tears ran down Lily's cheeks. She hurt *for* him and *with* him and couldn't even fathom living with his memories. She wrapped her arms around him, and he was rigid with resistance. Yet she kept holding on and wouldn't let go.

"Larry died," he said, his voice rough. "Larry died."

Leaning her head against his, she didn't even breathe. After what seemed like an eon, she murmured, "Don't send me away. Let me sleep here with you."

Whether Mitch was too exhausted to protest, too

awash in the past to care, he slid down under the covers, letting her hold on.

She didn't fall asleep again until she heard the deep, even rhythm of his breathing. Then she let herself slumber with him, knowing morning would come sooner than they both wanted.

Chapter Twelve

In the morning everything always looked different.

That's what Lily thought as she awakened, reached across the guest room bed and found that Mitch was gone.

He'd slept in the bed with her most of the night. She'd awakened a couple of times and cuddled close to him with her head on his shoulder. He'd been asleep then... she could tell. But something had made him leave now and she had to admit to herself that that was her biggest fear—that he would leave. If not physically, then emotionally.

Their physical reunion last night had been spectacular. What he'd shared with her about Iraq had been wrenching. Did he have regrets about that now? Was that why he'd left the bed?

She glanced at the clock and saw that it was 7:00 a.m.

She knew he was meeting his friends at the bed-and-breakfast for brunch, but that wasn't until ten o'clock. She caught up the flannel shirt she'd discarded last night and slipped it on. She'd shower and dress after she found out where Mitch had gone.

After she buttoned his shirt from neckline to hem, she realized how silly that was. She certainly hadn't been so modest last night. She'd never felt so wanton or so free…so hungry or so sexual.

Sunlight poured in the hall skylight, a new, bright December day with Christmas right around the corner. What gift could she get Mitch?

She hated feeling uncertain like this. She hated not knowing how deep his feelings ran. Were they just having an affair?

That possibility made her heartsick.

She smelled the aroma of coffee and heard Mitch's voice before she saw him. He was pacing the kitchen, talking on his cell phone. He went to the French doors and looked out as he listened.

Spotting his jacket around the kitchen chair, a mug of coffee half gone, she wondered if he'd sat outside this morning in the cold before he'd come in to make his phone call. Who was he talking to? Jimmy? Matt?

Then she heard him say, "Dr. Dolman, I appreciate what you're saying. I searched your articles online this morning." There was a pause. "Yes, that too. I trust Matt. But I wanted to check out your credentials for myself."

Dr. Dolman. The surgeon who could possibly repair Mitch's hand. If Mitch was going to talk to him, why hadn't he discussed it with her? Why had he disappeared from the bed without a "good morning" or a kiss? Last night had meant the world to her. Decisions they each made would affect the other's life. Unless they weren't really "together." Unless last night hadn't meant what she thought it did.

She felt hurt and knew she shouldn't. This was *his* life. This was *his* decision. But she did feel let down. She'd thought last night they'd gotten closer than any two people could get.

Mitch sensed her presence and turned, finding her in the doorway. For a moment their gazes met, but then his mind was on the conversation again and he looked away, shutting her out.

At least that's the way it felt. She wouldn't eavesdrop if he didn't want her there.

She returned to the master bedroom and bath, catching the scent of Mitch's soap still lingering in the shower. She'd thought maybe they could shower together this morning. She'd thought—

Stop it, she chastised herself. Disappointment pressed against her heart as she showered quickly, found a blow dryer under Mitch's sink and blew most of the wetness from her hair. She'd dressed and was picking up her own phone to call the Victorian when she heard Mitch coming down the hall.

She closed her phone and waited.

He saw her standing there with it in her hand. "How are the twins?"

"I don't know. I haven't called yet."

The intimacy they'd shared last night seemed to have been lost. The electric buzz between them was still there, but there was nothing comfortable about it. She kept quiet to let him choose the first topic for discussion.

He asked, "You overheard some of my conversation?"

"Not much. Just the name of the doctor Matt told you about last night."

"Dr. Dolman."

She nodded.

"I was up early, went outside and did a ton of thinking."

She wanted to ask, *About us?* But that obviously wasn't what was on his mind.

"I thought about everything Matt said. He thinks I have survivor guilt."

"Do you?" she asked.

"Hell, I don't know. But I did think about why I wouldn't want to get my hand fixed. Yes, there could be more damage. But it also has to do with the life change I made."

"In other words, why rock the boat?" she inquired.

"Exactly. Yet I've never been a half-measure person. Why in this?"

There were only about three feet between them but it seemed like so much more.

He went on. "Dr. Dolman's success rate is outstanding. I made an appointment with him for Tuesday afternoon."

Tuesday was Mitch's day off. He could reserve an early flight and be in Houston before noon.

"I see," she said.

Tilting his head, he studied her. "I thought you'd be happy about it."

She *was* terrifically pleased he'd made the decision. "I am. But why didn't you wake me up to talk about it? Why did you leave and cut off the closeness we'd shared? Why didn't you think I'd want to be part of whatever you decided?"

His back became straighter, his stance a little wider, as if he had a position to defend. "Why do you think?"

"I'm not at all sure."

"You're insightful, Lily. Take a guess."

"Mitch…"

"No woman has ever touched my scars. *You* did. No woman has ever seen me in the throes of one of my nightmares. *You* did. I never told a civilian back here what happened over there. But I told *you*. If I had stayed in that bed this morning and you'd opened your eyes and I'd seen pity or worse yet, dismay, that even after all these years I still haven't gotten a handle on my own subconscious—" He stopped abruptly. "I just didn't want to have to deal with that."

She didn't know what to say. There were so many levels to his statement. She didn't know how to separate it into all the aspects they needed to examine.

So she stated what was obvious to her. "Why would I feel pity? Mitch, you're a decorated hero. You were awarded a Silver Star, a Purple—"

"I'm *not* a hero. I didn't save Larry's life."

"No, but you tried. You risked *your* life."

"Results matter…in surgery, in helping couples conceive, in life."

Shaking her head, she sank down onto the corner of the bed, hoping he'd do the same. "You expect too much of yourself. And maybe you don't expect enough of me."

"Maybe that's because I think in your mind you're still married."

His words struck her hard and stole her breath. "Did I act like I was still married last night?"

"Did you feel guilt afterwards?"

"No, I didn't," she said almost angrily.

Then he looked down at her hand in her lap. "Then why are you still wearing your wedding ring?"

"This is about my *ring?* You're jealous because I can't forget my husband?"

"I'm *not* jealous," Mitch protested with a vehemence she almost believed. "It's not about that," he concluded. "It's about your ability to let go of Troy so you have something with me."

The thought of letting go of Troy absolutely panicked her! If she let go, didn't that mean their love hadn't been very strong? If she let go, didn't that mean Sophie and Grace would never know their real dad? If she let go, and Mitch left, what would she have then?

He must have seen the color drain from her face. He must have seen how shaken she was, because he covered the few feet between them and clasped her shoulder.

But his touch, which still sent scalding heat through her body, activated her. She stood and pulled away from him. "I have to go home to Sophie and Grace."

"I know you do." His voice had lost its edge and was gentler than she expected. "But this is something we've needed to discuss and haven't."

"I thought we were discussing your surgery." Her feelings for Mitch had been simpler when the focus was on *him.*

"If I have surgery, I'm doing it to move on. You say you want to move on, but I don't know if that's really true."

She was stymied for a response and didn't know what he wanted from her.

"Why don't you go home, get the twins and meet me at the bed-and-breakfast for brunch?"

"I don't think that's a good idea." The words reflexively spilled from her.

"Why not?"

"Because…because I don't know what kind of night they had. I don't know if they're fussy or content. I should have called first thing and I didn't."

"Why didn't you?" he probed.

Because you were on my mind, she thought. "Because you left and I didn't know why."

"I only went as far as the kitchen."

Maybe that was true, but it hadn't felt that way at the time.

"I need to go," she whispered. More than anything, she needed to hold Sophie and Grace. To kiss them. To feel the bond she had with them.

Seeming to understand that, Mitch nodded. "Okay. I'll help you carry your things to the car."

Lily felt shell-shocked…as if her whole world had just crashed in. Mitch had turned the tables so effectively she didn't know who was more conflicted…or which one of them could figure out where they could go from here.

On Tuesday evening Lily sat at the kitchen table with evergreen boughs, ribbon and gold bells spread across newspaper. She was making a wreath for the front door while Angie and Ellie added more Christmas touches to the rest of the house. The last time she'd looked they were arranging a nativity set on the table by the sofa.

When the phone rang, she called into them, "I'll get it," went to the counter and picked up the cordless. The caller ID simply read Out of Area without a number.

"Hello," she answered, afraid to hope the caller was Mitch. Yesterday he'd been busy at the office tying up loose ends, cramming appointments together, going over histories of his patients with Jon and Hillary in case he got tied up in Houston. When she'd asked him about the brunch, he'd said everyone hated to leave the bed-and-breakfast, but they all had to get back to their lives. He'd given her one of those "Mitch" looks that was intense and full of meaning.

But then Jon had buzzed him and he'd rushed off. He didn't seem to be shutting her out, yet he didn't seem to be waiting for anything from her, either.

Before she'd left for the day, she'd placed a note on his desk, wishing him luck.

"Lily, it's Mitch. Are you tied up?"

She wanted to say, *Yes, my stomach's tied in knots and I'm worried about you.* Instead, she replied, "Sophie and Grace are sleeping. Ellie, Angie and I are decorating."

"I wanted to let you know Dr. Dolman believes I'm a good candidate for surgery. He has a slot open on Friday afternoon, so I'm going to stay, have some tests and then let him operate."

"That soon?" she murmured.

"I had to make a decision, Lily. This surgery will either work or it won't. One way or another, I'll know, and I'll adjust my life accordingly."

That's what Mitch did. He adjusted his life to fit whatever happened to him. His history had shown her that. He was a decisive, confident man who didn't stall or procrastinate or wait…unless waiting fit into the big picture. How long would he wait for her? Maybe his patience had already come to an end.

"Anyway, I'm staying at the Longhorn Inn. Matt said I could crash at his place, but he's starting a three-day rotation and will be tied up. I wanted to give you the number where I'll be in case my cell is out of reach. Got a pen and paper?"

She grabbed a pen and tablet from the counter. "Go ahead." She jotted down the number he gave her. "How long will you be in Houston after your surgery?"

"I'll be discharged the next day, but Matt wants me to give it forty-eight hours until I fly. If all goes well, I'll be back Monday. I can do physical therapy in Lubbock."

If all goes well.

"What about after you're discharged? Doesn't someone have to be with you?"

"I'll be fine, Lily. Matt said he'll have one of his doc friends check on me."

She hated the fact Mitch was going through this practically alone. Like most men, he probably didn't want anyone to see him when he wasn't at his best. But she didn't like the idea he'd be alone after surgery. She didn't like the idea that he was in Houston alone now.

After a long silence, Mitch asked, "So, did you put up a Christmas tree?"

"Yes, we did. Complete with a lighted star on top. Sophie and Grace haven't seen it yet, though. When they wake up they won't know what to think."

"You're lucky they're not walking yet. You can still keep most things out of their reach."

"Except for the tree. Angie hung ornaments that wouldn't break on the bottom. I have a feeling they'll have a few tantrums until they realize they can't touch it."

"They have to learn boundaries."

There was a commotion on Mitch's end. "Someone's at my door, Lily. It's probably room service."

"You're just having dinner?"

"After the consultation, I talked to Matt and then drove around for a while. I needed to…think. I wasn't hungry then. But after I got back and showered, the idea of food sounded good."

"I won't keep you then."

"I'm sorry you're going to have a heavier load this week because of my being away."

"Don't be concerned about that, Mitch. Hillary and Jon and I will be fine."

"Okay, then. If you need anything, or have any questions about my patients, just call."

"I will. And Mitch, I'll be praying for you…that everything goes well."

"Thanks, Lily."

When his phone clicked off, she set down hers, the hollow feeling inside her seeming to echo with Mitch's voice.

Angie came into the kitchen and saw Lily standing there, staring at the phone. "What's going on?"

Lily told her about Mitch's consultation and surgery. "He shouldn't be there alone," Lily murmured when she was finished.

"Who should be with him?" Angie asked.

Lily knew what Angie was suggesting. "I have Grace and Sophie to think about. And the practice."

"Take them with you."

Suddenly Lily heard a cry from the baby monitor.

"That's Grace," she said. "I'll find out what's wrong." On her way out of the kitchen, she glanced back at Angie. "I feel pulled in so many directions. I can't think about going to Houston. At least not tonight."

"Tomorrow will come soon enough," her housemate suggested.

Lily knew she was right.

On the way home from the office on Wednesday, Lily took a detour. After arriving at the outskirts of Sagebrush, she turned down a road where she hadn't driven for over a year…almost sixteen months. Mid-December darkness had already fallen and she glimpsed farms along the road with Christmas decorations and lights twinkling from eaves, gables and shrubs in front yards.

Eventually Lily reached an illuminated lane where a security guard was housed in a cupola before a high fence. She presented ID to him and a key. After a few taps into his computer, he okayed her, opened the gate and let her drive inside.

She passed row upon row of storage compartments, some looking more like closets, some the size of a garage. The area was well lit and there were no other cars around. It didn't take her long to find the row, and then the storage compartment that she was looking for. She didn't think as she parked in front of it. She tried not to feel. If she let herself feel now, what would happen after she went inside?

She did check her watch and knew she couldn't spend a whole lot of time here. Not today anyway. Sophie and Grace were waiting for her.

After she unlocked the combination, she inserted the

key into the padlock. Two levels of security. Now both were just barriers, locking her out of memories that she'd stored because they were too painful to see, listen to or handle.

The roll-up door stuck and she wondered if she'd have to call the security guard to help her heave it up. But then it gave way and rolled open, revealing the remnants of her marriage. At least the physical ones.

Stepping into the past, she looked around and her eyes burned. It was the cold, the staleness of the compartment, the boxes upon boxes that almost sixteen months ago she couldn't bear to donate or toss away. Moving to the Victorian had accomplished more than giving her an economical place to live, friends to support her, room for her twins to grow. Moving there so quickly after Troy had died had removed her from a good dose of the pain of losing him. She'd been nearly numb when she'd packed up her belongings and his. She'd sent a lot of Troy's things home to his mother, knowing she'd treasure them. But the rest was here in front of her, making her eyes go misty with the remembrance of what was inside the boxes.

She could sit here and go through them one by one. They were labeled and she knew what she'd find. But she hadn't come here to open a box with souvenirs from her Caribbean honeymoon with Troy or CDs they'd once listened to together. She'd come here to find something that would tell her whether she could meld the past with the present…if she *could* really move on. Besides cartons, she had to step over and around Troy's saws and metal boxes that held sets of chisels or a Dremel tool. Finally, after she'd moved a circular saw housed on its own table, she found what she was looking for in the corner.

She had asked Troy to make this for her. It was a multi-tiered plant stand fashioned in oak. Almost finished, it simply needed a last smoothing with fine sandpaper, polishing and then a coat of acrylic.

At least three feet high, the plant stand was bulky as she pushed it from its protected place to the front of the storage compartment and ran her hands over it, imagining Troy doing the same. Now tears really pressed against her eyelids. Giving in, she let them come and didn't even try to brush them away.

When she heard a sound, she realized an airplane was buzzing overhead. At the edge of the compartment, she lifted her gaze to the sky. The moon was bright, almost full, and brought back the memory of standing at the fire pit on Mitch's patio singing "Silent Night." Her nose was numb. Her fingers were stiff. Her feet were cold in her high-heeled pumps. But the cold didn't matter now as she stood still, just letting every feeling in her life wash over her.

Her gaze lifted to the moon and she suddenly saw something to the east of it—a shooting star. It glowed, streaked, then vanished.

Like Troy?

Turning away from the sky, she ran her hands over the solid wood again. She heard the question in her head as if someone were standing in the compartment speaking to her. *Do you love Mitch?*

Searching for the answer here, in the midst of her past life, she knew she did.

Why? that little voice asked again. *Because I asked him to look out for you?*

Reverently she slid her hands over the oak grain, straight and crooked, with imperfections and beauty despite that. She and Troy and Mitch had imperfections and beauty, too. No, she didn't love Mitch because Troy had asked him to watch over her. She loved Mitch because of who he was, and who she was when she was with him. She loved him because he was passionate and intense, and tender and caring. She loved him differently than she'd loved Troy. Whether or not that was because of Sophie and Grace, she didn't know. All of a sudden she just knew her love for Mitch was right.

Yes, it had come along at a time when she was still grieving. And maybe she'd miss Troy for the rest of her life. Loss wouldn't go away merely because she wanted it to. But Troy had so often told her, *There are no coincidences*. On and off, over the past nine months, she'd tested what she'd felt for Mitch. And every time, the desire, the aching to be with him, the dreams that appeared when she let herself think about the future couldn't be denied.

With one hand on the plant stand, she looked down at her other hand, where her wedding ring gleamed in the white moonlight. She slipped it off her finger and set it on the top shelf of the stand.

It was then that she felt warmth seeping into her body, as if someone had given her a giant hug. The sensation only lasted a matter of moments. Then once again she felt her cold nose, her stiff fingers, her numbing feet. She picked up the ring and slipped it into a zippered pocket in her purse. Then she pushed the plant stand out of the storage compartment, determined to fit it into her car.

She had to get home to Sophie and Grace and make an airline reservation to Houston.

Chapter Thirteen

The nurse ran the IV and Mitch watched the drip. This surgery was really going to happen.

Although Matt had stopped in a little while before, the one person Mitch wanted to talk to was Lily. But she was back in Sagebrush.

When the nurse left Mitch's cubicle, he flexed both hands, staring at his right one. Someday in the future, if not able to perform surgery, he might have fuller use of his fingers. Would he feel whole if he did?

He doubted it. Because he realized now he didn't need the use of his fingers to feel whole. He needed Lily. That need had been supremely evident the night of the reunion when they'd made love. Somehow, on that night, attraction and chemistry had transformed into something else entirely.

It had transformed into love.

He hadn't had the courage to admit it or the courage to feel it until he'd awakened the following morning holding her. Yet at that same moment he'd had doubts about Lily's ability to love again...doubts about her ability to freely make any kind of commitment to him. If he pushed her, he'd lose her.

He'd almost lost her when his ego had slid between them in June and his pride had convinced him to put time and distance between them. He'd almost lost her again when he'd prodded her about her wedding ring on Sunday morning.

Would she cut and run? Would she decide loving Troy for the rest of her life was enough? Were her feelings not deep enough to allow a future to develop between them?

He wanted her here to talk about all of it—his past mistakes, his future possibilities, her independence, their passionate hunger that went deeper than pheromones. He hadn't asked her to come, because she had Sophie and Grace to consider first. He hadn't asked her to come, because he knew if he pushed too hard she'd slip away entirely.

Turning away from the IV stand, he closed his eyes and tried to blank his mind.

Lily rushed down the hospital corridor hoping she wasn't too late. She had to see Mitch before he went into surgery. She *had* to.

The past three days had felt like a global marathon.

When she'd returned from the storage unit, Ellie had helped her carry in the plant stand. She'd also noticed the absent wedding ring. When Lily had explained what she wanted to do, Ellie had offered to take care of Sophie and Grace while she went to Houston. Angie had been at home, too, and when Lily couldn't find available seating on a flight, she'd called her brother-in-law, billionaire Logan Barnes. He'd booked Lily first-class seats. Both Angie and Ellie convinced her the twins would be well taken care of. Lily didn't have to worry about anything... except what Mitch was going to say and do.

Now as Lily headed for the information desk in the surgical wing, she was afraid. She loved Mitch Cortega with all her heart. But what if he'd lost patience with her? What if she was too late? What if he rejected her and she'd made a fool of herself?

She kept going anyway, almost at a jog. If she made a fool of herself, so be it.

When she reached the desk and inquired about Mitch's whereabouts, the woman asked, "Are you family?"

Lily said blithely, "I'm his fiancée."

Narrowing her eyes, the clerk asked if Lily knew his date of birth.

"I do. It's January twenty-first."

A tad less warily, the gatekeeper of this surgical unit next asked for his home address and telephone number.

Resigned to this delay, Lily rattled them off.

Finally the clerk pointed her in the direction she should go, advising, "Follow the yellow floor line."

Doing so, Lily almost ran toward the surgical waiting area, found cubicle number six and peeked around the curtain.

There Mitch was, lying on a gurney, an IV line attached to the hand that wouldn't be undergoing surgery.

She wondered if he'd already been given medication to relax, if he'd even be aware that she was here.

Crossing to the bed, she stood beside it and asked softly, "Mitch?"

His eyes opened. They were clear, alert and totally flabbergasted. "Lily? What are you doing here? My surgery was delayed an hour and they haven't given me anything yet. So I know you can't be a hallucination." He sat up and looked ready to climb out of the bed.

She laid a hand on his shoulder, stood as close as she could without jumping into bed with him, then plunged in. "I had to see you in person. I had to tell you before you went into surgery."

"What? Did something happen to Sophie or Grace?" The lines on his forehead cutting deep, his expression showed his extreme worry.

"They're fine. Ellie and Angie are taking good care of them."

Now he just looked totally perplexed.

She took his hand, stroked the scars on his arm and gazed deeply into his eyes. "I love you, Mitch. I couldn't let you go into surgery not knowing that. You've been so patient and I don't know if that patience has run out or not. But I do love you. I want to be with you. I want a future with you."

He didn't look as ecstatic as she thought he might, as she'd *hoped* he might. Instead, he looked troubled. "What happened, Lily?"

He didn't believe her! In fact, he seemed to consider her appearance as impulsive, that she might change her mind tomorrow. She stayed close to him, her hand still on his arm. Somehow she'd make him understand. "I went to the storage compartment where I kept everything

I didn't move into the Victorian. Troy's tools are there, and the plant stand he made for me before he was deployed."

Mitch began to say something but she didn't give him the chance. She rushed on. "The stand isn't finished and I'd like to finish it. And then I want to put it in your sunroom where it can hold plants or flowers and remind me of the love Troy gave me. It's part of my past, Mitch. Troy is part of my past. And I'll always hold his memory dear in my heart. I don't think it was a coincidence he chose you to look after me. He used to say, 'There are no coincidences,' and I believe he was right. When I was standing there looking at the moon and spotting a shooting star—I'd never seen one before in my life—I remembered standing by the fire pit with you and singing 'Silent Night.' My whole being just understood I should finally admit what I've been feeling. I *do* love you, Mitch Cortega. I'm ready to commit to you for the rest of my life. If you aren't ready, that's okay. We'll figure things out as we go. *Together.*"

She could see that what she was saying and feeling and meaning took a few moments for Mitch to absorb. But then he opened his arms to her. "Come here."

She didn't hesitate. If someone came in to take him to surgery, they could just take her along, too!

On his lap, with his arms around her the best he could manage it, he kissed her with such soul-stirring passion she thought she'd melt right into him.

But then he broke the kiss and lifted his head. "When we made love Saturday night, I was forced to admit to myself I was doing a hell of a lot more than watching over you. I hadn't tried the word *love* on what I felt. But on Sunday, I did. I guess I was embarrassed after the bad dream. I woke up thinking I had to do *something*. If you weren't ready, then I had to prepare myself for whatever life dealt. The best way to do that was to see if I could have my hand repaired."

"I was hurt you didn't talk about it with me," she admitted, knowing she had to be honest with him about everything.

"I'm sorry. I guess I thought I'd given you too many pieces of myself and this was one I had to take control of."

Stroking his face, she said, "I want all of you, Mitch. Not just the strong parts or the perfect parts. I'll support you no matter what happens, whether we return to our practice or whether you want to go back to trauma surgery. And I have no intention of moving to Oklahoma. I'm staying in Sagebrush with *you*."

Taking Lily's hand, Mitch smiled. "This isn't the place I'd imagined we'd be talking about this. I want to give you romance and flowers and music to remember the day by, not the clanging of hospital trays. But it seems like I've waited for you for so long, and I don't want to wait a second longer. Will you marry me?"

"When?" She'd be ready today if that's what he wanted.

"Soon. As soon as we can fly back to Sagebrush and arrange it. I don't want to wait a minute more than I have to to be your husband. And," he hesitated, then continued, "a stepfather to Sophie and Grace."

"You're not going to be a *step*father. You're going to be their dad. Troy would want that. I know he would."

Mitch kissed her again, just as the nurse swung back the curtain.

They were oblivious, lost in passion and promises they yearned to share.

Epilogue

"This is as unconventional as it gets," Mitch murmured to Lily, folding his arm around her in her cream wool cape. As long as she was in his arms, the world was good and he slept peacefully during the deep night hours. Marriage would gift them with the future they both wanted and needed.

Twinkle lights were strung around the border of Mitch's patio. The fire pit was lit, giving off warmth. The minister from Lily's church had agreed to perform the service. He'd told her early evening was fine. Afterward, he could return to his congregation for Christmas Eve midnight service.

Fortunately, the weather had cooperated and even Mitch had to admit his patio looked wedding-ready. The stars were crystal clear and the slice of moon glowed with silver-white light. An arbor, also decorated in evergreens and twinkle lights, housed the minister as Lily and Mitch stood before him, ready to say their vows.

Lily cast a glance at Ellie, who was holding Grace, and at Angie, who was carrying Sophie. The twins were bundled up in their pink snowsuits and mittens, their noses barely peeking out from their hoods. Gina had dressed Daniel similarly in blue, and Logan held his son so he could see what was going on, too, as Eva stood with Hannah ready to help with the kids. Shep and Raina had brought along Joey, Roy and Manuel. Tessa and her husband, Vince, held their children's hands, while Francesca and Grady as well as Emily and Jared stood by with their children. Within driving distance, Tony and Jimmy had brought their wives, children and Christmas along with them. Beside them, Lily and Mitch's colleagues watched from along one stone wall where the twinkle lights flickered high above them.

Lily had wanted them all here to witness this joyous celebration. She loved Mitch so much she wanted everyone who could to share their joy. They'd only be outside for about ten minutes and then they'd go inside for their reception, which would be homey and all theirs.

In a low voice beside Mitch, Matt said, "You two couldn't wait until spring, could you?"

Mitch shook his head. "Not a chance. You and I both know each day is a precious gift, and I want to spend them all with Lily."

Lily cuddled closer to Mitch, not at all cold, just wanting to feel him near. He was wearing a black, Western-cut leather jacket. His hand and wrist were still bandaged. After Christmas they would fly back to Houston for an exam by the doctor and decide whether

Mitch was ready for physical therapy. The surgery had gone well, but it might take time for him to have use of those fingers again.

Reverend Allbright made some opening remarks and then said, "I understand the two of you have vows to make to each other."

"We do," they said in unison.

"Whoever wants to go first," the kindly older man invited.

Lily took Mitch's hands, one bandaged and one not, in both of hers. "I know how important vows and promises are to you. I promise to love you from morning till night and every minute in between. I vow to be your partner, lover and friend and I will always respect your opinion in raising our girls. Each and every day, I will try to bring happiness into your life and will be proud to call you my husband."

Mitch cleared his throat and held on to her as tightly as she was holding on to him. "I was broken when I met you, in ways I didn't even understand. Your acceptance, passion and caring have changed that. Having you and Sophie and Grace in my life has healed past wounds. I want nothing more than to be your husband and their dad. You are everything I've ever wanted, the woman I didn't even know I hoped to find. I love you, Lily, and I will cherish you, protect you, honor and respect you every day of our lives."

The minister opened his hand to Lily. Raina handed her a wide gold band and Lily placed it in the minister's hand. Matt handed Mitch a circle of diamonds and Mitch placed that in the minister's palm, also.

Reverend Allbright said, "These rings embody the circle of love that you have promised each other. I give them to you now to slide onto each other's fingers in memory of this night, the vows you have made and the love you will share."

Lily took the ring again and slid it onto Mitch's finger. "I thee wed," she said solemnly.

Mitch took the ring from the minister's hand and slid it onto Lily's finger. "I thee wed," he echoed, just as solemnly.

They held hands and faced forward again.

Reverend Allbright smiled. "I now pronounce you husband and wife."

Mitch took Lily into his arms and she lifted her face to his. Their kiss was an embodiment of everything their ceremony had entailed.

When Mitch raised his head, he said loud and clear, "I love you."

She kissed him again and buried her nose by his ear. "I love you, too."

Everyone around them was applauding and they realized they weren't alone in the universe. With her husband beside her, Lily went to Grace and lifted her into her arms. Mitch did the same with Sophie and they came together for a group hug.

"Can we cut the cake now?" Joey asked.

"We can cut the cake," Mitch announced happily, tickling Sophie.

After more hugs all around, they headed into Mitch's house, ready to begin their lives and the future they would build together.

* * * * *

Look for Karen Rose Smith's REUNION BRIDES series,
Coming soon to Silhouette Special Edition!

COMING NEXT MONTH

Available December 28, 2010

SPECIAL EDITION

HARLEQUIN®

A Romance

FOR EVERY MOOD™

Spotlight on

Classic

Quintessential, modern love stories
that are romance at its finest.

See the next page
to enjoy a sneak peek from
the Harlequin Presents® series.

*Harlequin Presents® is thrilled
to introduce the first installment of
an epic tale of passion and drama by*
**USA TODAY Bestselling Author
Penny Jordan!**

*When buttoned-up Giselle first meets
the devastatingly handsome Saul Parenti,
the heat between them is explosive....*

"LET ME GET THIS STRAIGHT. Are you actually suggesting that I would stoop to that kind of game playing?"

Saul came out from behind his desk and walked toward her. Giselle could smell his hot male scent and it was making her dizzy, igniting a low, dull, pulsing ache that was taking over her whole body.

Giselle defended her suspicions. "You don't want me here."

"No," Saul agreed, "I don't."

And then he did what he had sworn he would not do, cursing himself beneath his breath as he reached for her, pulling her fiercely into his arms and kissing her with all the pent-up fury she had aroused in him from the moment he had first seen her.

Giselle certainly *wanted* to resist him. But the hand she raised to push him away developed a will of its own and was sliding along his bare arm beneath the sleeve of his shirt, and the body that should have been arching away from him was instead melting into him.

Beneath the pressure of his kiss he could feel and taste her gasp of undeniable response to him. He wanted to devour her, take her and drive them both until they were equally satiated—even whilst the anger within him that she should make him feel that way roared and burned its resentment of his need.

She was helpless, Giselle recognized, totally unable to withstand the storm lashing at her, able only to cling to the man who was the cause of it and pray that she would survive.

Somewhere else in the building a door banged. The sound exploded into the sensual tension that had enclosed them, driving them apart. Saul's chest was rising and falling as he fought for control; Giselle's whole body was trembling.

Without a word she turned and ran.

Find out what happens when Saul and Giselle succumb to their irresistible desire in

THE RELUCTANT SURRENDER

Available January 2011 from Harlequin Presents®

REQUEST YOUR FREE BOOKS!
2 FREE NOVELS PLUS 2 FREE GIFTS!

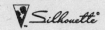

SPECIAL EDITION
Life, Love and Family!

YES! Please send me 2 FREE Silhouette® Special Edition® novels and my 2 FREE gifts (gifts are worth about $10). After receiving them, if I don't wish to receive any more books, I can return the shipping statement marked "cancel." If I don't cancel, I will receive 6 brand-new novels every month and be billed just $4.24 per book in the U.S. or $4.99 per book in Canada. That's a saving of 15% off the cover price! It's quite a bargain! Shipping and handling is just 50¢ per book.* I understand that accepting the 2 free books and gifts places me under no obligation to buy anything. I can always return a shipment and cancel at any time. Even if I never buy another book from Silhouette, the two free books and gifts are mine to keep forever.

235/335 SDN E5RG

Name _____ (PLEASE PRINT) _____

Address _____ Apt. #

City _____ State/Prov. _____ Zip/Postal Code

Signature (if under 18, a parent or guardian must sign)

Mail to the **Silhouette Reader Service:**
IN U.S.A.: P.O. Box 1867, Buffalo, NY 14240-1867
IN CANADA: P.O. Box 609, Fort Erie, Ontario L2A 5X3

Not valid for current subscribers to Silhouette Special Edition books.

Want to try two free books from another line?
Call 1-800-873-8635 or visit www.morefreebooks.com.

* Terms and prices subject to change without notice. Prices do not include applicable taxes. N.Y. residents add applicable sales tax. Canadian residents will be charged applicable provincial taxes and GST. Offer not valid in Quebec. This offer is limited to one order per household. All orders subject to approval. Credit or debit balances in a customer's account(s) may be offset by any other outstanding balance owed by or to the customer. Please allow 4 to 6 weeks for delivery. Offer available while quantities last.

Your Privacy: Silhouette is committed to protecting your privacy. Our Privacy Policy is available online at www.eHarlequin.com or upon request from the Reader Service. From time to time we make our lists of customers available to reputable third parties who may have a product or service of interest to you. If you would prefer we not share your name and address, please check here. ☐

Help us get it right—We strive for accurate, respectful and relevant communications. To clarify or modify your communication preferences, visit us at www.ReaderService.com/consumerchoice.

SSE10R